I0650921

JUMPER ORIGINS

Evan JAMES Vaughan

Edited by Betty Norlin

JUMPER ORIGINS

Evan James Vaughan

Copyright @ 2025, Evan James Vaughan

All rights reserved. No part of this book may be reproduced, stored, or transmitted by any means—whether auditory, graphic, mechanical, or electronic—without written permission of both publisher and author, except in the case of brief excerpts used in critical articles and reviews. Unauthorized reproduction of any part of this work is illegal and punishable by law.

Because of the dynamic nature of the Internet, any web addresses or links contained in this book may have changed since publication and may no longer be valid.

Paperback (standard color): 978-1-7363617-9-5
Paperback (black and white interior): 979-8-9998412-7-8
eBook Kindle: ISBN: 979-8-9998412-4-7
eBook EPUB: 979-8-9998412-5-4

First edition published in 2025. Published in the United States. Written by a human without AI assistance.

Published in the United States by:

What is Holistic Health, LLC, Tampa, Florida

To my friends Tripp & Valerio,
Without them I wouldn't have made this book.

TABLE OF CONTENTS

Introduction

Jumper Origins has been on my mind for the longest time. I have never truly felt I have perfected it until this point. It has been a rough journey trying to discover what the true story of this book should be. Not to mention the characters, and other aspects too. However, after many years working on and off on this book, I can confidently confirm that I am satisfied with it.

Jumper Origins is a very complex book. It is filled with references, concepts, and ideas inspired by video games. The story follows a large array of fictional events, documented by the two main protagonists, Eop of Ping-Pong and Jumper of Watch Base 01.

Eop and Jumper lived in the video game world. A world that was created by Humans. This world is divided among two factions: Game Protectors (a group Humans created to combat Glitches within video games), and Glitches (also referred to as Ethites). Both protagonists wind up in the middle of this conflict. Eop (a Playable Character within the video game Ping-

Pong) ends up becoming a Game Protector, and Jumper (a Game Protector who is simultaneously a Glitch) is seemingly a prophet destined to create peace between the two parties. And although they are generations apart, Eop and Jumper's lives end up intertwined, in order to change their world.

Prologue

Black. Utter darkness. That is how our world began. Then, The Developers appeared. But who are The Developers? Humans. But who are The Humans? Humans are an advanced race, and in fact, they are much like us. They too have emotions, have lives, and people in which they care deeply about. That includes us. Humans also have distinct personalities from one another, they have different interests, and they disagree, much like us. Above all these qualities, Humans are creators. Creators of entertainment, technology, and much more. Beyond all of this, they created us: life within a simulation, crafted by programming. This, The Humans called a "Video Game." However, not every Human knows the secrets that go into programming. Therefore, we made a distinction. Those who created us are called "The Developers," and those who did not, are simply referred to as "Humans."

But what was the purpose of video games? Of our creation? This is a question we ask daily. In truth, video games were created to offer entertainment, and an escape from reality to The Humans. An escape like no other. One where The Humans could both access and interact with a virtual world around them. They could experience a world they had never seen before.

But how? How did they access and interact with this new world? Playable Characters.

In the beginning, there were only two "Playable Characters" in existence. Their names were: Lee-Der and Eop.

To those unfamiliar with the term "Playable Characters," it applies to the beings in which The Humans can control. In this day and age, The Developers have created many different methods in which they can control these characters. The method available in the beginning was a box, with a small screen, some buttons, and a joystick. This box was called an "Arcade Machine." Every input a human made using this device would control a different aspect of a Playable Character. For instance, a Human could use the joystick to move a Playable Character around. This, however, did not mean that Playable Characters were without free will. If, for instance, a Playable Character was not currently being controlled, they could move independently. Beyond movement, Playable Characters could also communicate and talk with each other. However, the conversations they could have were quite limited—and primitive. Of course, this would later change. But how did they speak, and move, on their own without The Humans noticing? The Filterveil, and code. The latter is what will be discussed next.

Code was the name of the language in which Playable Characters used to communicated. This language was quite unique, as no Human, at least not an average Human, could read it. In fact, no Human could actually speak it. The dialogue of code is inaudible to Human ears, and therefore it seemed as if Playable Characters never spoke.

The Filterveil was what obscured the inner workings of video games to most Humans. The Filterveil insured that no Human would see a Playable Character do something that was not programmed in their game. The Filterveil is the reasoning for loading screens, and it is even responsible for earlier games having poorer graphics. Due to the fact that earlier games were smaller, had less space, less areas to hold data, the Filterveil had to obscure things even more, causing older games to look more pixelated than the games of today, at least, to The Humans. Once video games got larger, and more space was implemented, there were more places to put the data, and therefore the Filterveil didn't have to obscure nearly as much. This resulted in the quality of graphics improving. That still begs the question though. Was there really too much data in one game, that the Filterveil really had to hide it? Not exactly. Data was not the only issue, for the Filterveil also had to disguise programming.

But why? Why must programming be hidden, or at least hidden to some degree? While it is true that programming makes up everything in our world, including our kind, and even our personalities, at its most basic form, it is just letters and numbers. The Filterveil is what gives programming its shape and makes it more than just a bunch of symbols. It disguises programming into a world, in a place in which Humans can escape their reality. But to us, this is our reality.

With all that stated, the last topic of this introduction can be explained.

Eop and Lee-Der were created to be the first Playable Characters in the video game, entitled "Ping-Pong." Everything about Eop and Lee-Der were primitive. Their minds, the actions they could perform, and their design. Due to the Filterveil, Humans could only see Eop and Lee-Der as two white blocks called "pixels." It is for this reason that The Developers opted to give Eop and Lee-Der simpler designs. These designs consisted of a fully white body, with a small head fitted with black eyes and an empty black mouth, a slim and scrawny chest, a pair of massive arms, as well as a pair of massive legs. These physical features will give them the speed, and agility, to be able to play Ping-Pong. As for their personalities, Eop tended to be peaceful, as well as curious about life, among other things. He also was quite clever and smart. He enjoyed playing Ping-Pong both with and without Human control, and didn't give too much care if he won or lost against Lee-Der. On the other hand, Lee-Der was almost the complete opposite. He tended to be very competitive, very angsty, and sometimes angry. However, there was no denying that Lee-Der had an amazing ability of being persuasive, as well as outsmarting any foe that he faced. That is why whenever Eop and Lee-Der played Ping-Pong without Human control, Lee-Der always won.

Ping-Pong was dark, and very barren. There was no ground, no sky, and it was almost just utter black darkness. In the exact middle of Ping-Pong, there were two white poles, with a net stretching across them. This net had a pattern of many small octagon-shaped holes throughout it, allowing Eop and Lee-Der to clearly see each other. Additionally, the poles and the net had endless altitude, reaching endlessly down, and endlessly up. Lee-Der and Eop were never able to have any physical contact. Even with the small holes in the net, they could not seem to find a way to force their arms through the net, in order to shake hands before a game of Ping-Pong.

Due to the Filterveil however, Humans saw the net as a couple of white pixels, with black gaps in-between each white pixel.

Other than the net, there were only two other objects in Ping-Pong. The first was the ball. This ball was white, with two separate black lines wrapping around the ball on the left and right sides. Unfortunately, the Filterveil obscured these details, making the Ping-Pong ball appear as a one single white pixel. This ball was very firm, and yet could bounce quite easily, making it easy to initiate a game of Ping-Pong. The last object in Ping-Pong was the two white numbers. One was suspended above Eop's head, and the other suspended above Lee-Der's head. These numbers were suspended by a thin black rope. One number represented the number of points Eop scored, and the other represented the amount of points Lee-Der scored. Once either character scored, the number above their head would change, via an automatic rope-and-pulley system. However, this system was so swift, that it almost appeared as if the numbers just changed on their own. It did not help that the Filterveil obscured the rope-and-pulley system to The Humans.

But what was a game of Ping-Pong? With every object and/or person in the game explained, that question can now be answered. Ping-Pong is a game in which The Human can take control of either Eop or Lee-Der and control them using a joystick. Once the game was started, the Ping-Pong ball would begin to bounce, and The Human would use Eop or Lee-Der to try and block the Ping-Pong ball from getting behind their Playable Character, as well as try to get the Ping-Pong ball behind their opponent. If The Human managed to get the ball behind their opponent, they would earn a point. If their opponent managed to do this, the opponent would earn a point. Who is the opponent though? The opponent is whichever character The Human is not currently controlling. In this case, the uncontrolled character acts on his own free will in order to play against The Human.

There is also an option for two Humans to control Playable Characters and play Ping-Pong against each other, where one Human plays as Eop, and one plays as Lee-Der. In this case, neither Playable Character acts on their own free will.

Lee-Der and Eop's Argument, August 7, 1974

"Lee-Der!" Eop smiled, "I feel as if we have not seen each other all day! How are you, my friend?" Eop greeted, "I am bored, Eop. I feel... forgotten. Forgotten by The Humans, by The Developers," Lee-Der admitted.

"I understand that. It seems as though The Humans do not play Ping-Pong anymore."

Lee-Der shook his head, "It is not fair that we be forgotten, that we become a distant memory. That we, their creations, be ignored as they move on to other deeds."

"I sense agitation in your voice," Eop noticed.

"I am agitated, Eop!" Lee-Der turned to face his friend. "This might seem brash, but I do not think The Humans deserve to create. All they do is forge ahead and forget, making us feel neglected," Lee-Der snarled.

"Lee-Der..." Eop felt sorrow for his friend, "I am sure that The Developers nor The Humans; have forgotten of us. Though they seem far away, they are with us. They are all around us. Just look at the world they made for us. They may have moved on to greater things for now, but our spirit is still with them," Eop reassured.

Lee-Der's Battle With The Game Protectors, August 7, 1974

"It is still not right, Eop. That we be forgotten by The Humans. By even our creators, The Developers," Lee-Der sighed, "I regret in saying this...but I am beginning to believe there are no Developers. No so-called Humans."

"How could you say that?" Eop asked in disbelief, "This whole time we have felt their presence through us," Eop waved his hand across the sky. "Seen in their creation. Are we not enough proof that they exist?"

"Yes, but there could be another way...another way to explain all of this."

"Perhaps. But does it not take more faith to believe in no creator; instead of believing there is one?"

Lee-Der thought a moment, but his thoughts were interrupted, as a tearing-like sound ripped the sky open like a page of a book.

Eop and Lee-Der looked to the sky and saw a dark silhouette of what seemed to be more of their kind, dropping out from the hole in the sky. Each silhouette landed on the ground beneath them, looking eerily identical.

"Lee-Der. Of. Ping-Pong. By. The. Authority. Of. The. Game. Protectors., And. The. Developers., You. Have. Been. Sentenced. To. Life. Imprisonment." One of the silhouettes, now clear as day, stated. He looked wise and fresh. His armor and skin were a shinning gray, just like a moon at night. He was also fairly taller than the others; presumably making him the commander.

"What crime have I committed?" Lee-Der asked.

"It. Is. Not. A. matter. Of. What. Crime. You. Have.

Committed., But. Rather., What. Crime. You. Could. Commit. After all, you are a Glitch, and you are a grand threat."

"Glitch? What are you talking about?" Lee-Der grew confused.

"I. Grow. Tired. Of. Your. Games. Ethite., You. Know. Precisely. What. You. Are., And. Now....So. Do. We. Arrest. Him!"

The other beings surrounding their commander charged at Lee-Der. Though he tried his best, railing his arms to block their attacks, their tactics were too grand for him to overcome.

"Eop! Please! Help me!" Lee-Der gasped in fear.

Eop stood watching his friend. He was motionless, and in mere shock; slowly being traumatized by the events ahead of him.

The Arrest of Lee-Der, August 7, 1974

Lee-Der screamed out in a booming, furious, and pronounced voice: "We were friends once!" Lee-Der jerked his head back to look back at Eop who was behind him: "We are that no longer!" Lee-Der cried out in a fit of rage, and then he brought his head back to the front of his body.

Eop stood there, his expression soulless. He had just lost the greatest ally he had ever had. Eop moved his head down in sorrow, and he closed his eyes. Eop was unable to process the simple emotion of sadness, unable to confidently say what was wrong with him. When a Game Protector noticed Eop, he asked in a monotone, emotionless voice: "What. Are. You. Doing?" Eop looked at the Game Protector. He was on his left,

"I....suppose I do not know," Eop said, his voice almost sounding more evolved, more so full of emotion, full of what he would call sadness.

That same Game Protector, the one Eop would later be introduced formally to, was "0-1." This Game Protector was large, commanding. From one glance, you would immediately know him to be in charge. Like the other Game Protectors though, he lacked a proper distinction of armor. He too was just a simple light gray. If height, and stature, did not exist, 0-1 would just be like the others.

Eop was ushered away by 0-2, who put his hand on Eop's back, and started slowly walking: "This. Will. Be. Sorted. Out. Soon." 0-2 stated chillingly, offering barely any real comfort to Eop. Eop again looked down to the ground, staring at his feet. The Game Protectors, Lee-Der, and Eop then walked up to the portal that had opened up from before.

"Where are you taking us?" Eop questioned.

"Watch. Base. 01. Located. In. Superworld." And they all went through the portal.

The Journey to Watch Base 01, August 7, 1974

The wind gusted a loud roar and pushed against the trotting forces of Eop and The Game Protectors. "What is this place?" Eop asked.

"This. Is. Superworld. A. Blank. Canvas. For. A. Future. Game!" 0-1 yelled over the howling winds, "It. Seems. As. Though. The. Developers. Are. Testing. The. Weather. System."

Eop blocked the wind from coming upon him by placing his arm on his forehead. After much wind, resistance, and trouble; The Game Protectors, Eop, and Lee-Der finally made it to the armored silver gates of Watch Base 01.

0-1, being the largest and strongest of The Game Protectors, proceeded to forcefully slide both doors open; and then stepped inside the base, moving aside to let all of the others in. Once everyone was inside, 0-1 then forcefully closed the doors, sealing away the wind.

"Take. The. Glitch. To. The. Holding. Cells. And. See. To. Eop's. injuries. If. He. Received. Any." 0-1 commanded.

0-3 nodded, and ushered Eop to come with him. Eop's face was full of surprise, confusion, and a mix of many emotions.

The Question of Eop, August 7, 1974

The room Eop and 0-3 entered was vast yet empty-looking. The only objects that lined the walls were drawers; many of them in fact containing medical-related supplies. In the center was a rectangular-like structure, elevated off the ground by small silver poles only a few inches high.

"Put. Yourself. On. That. Resting. Spot. Then. Lay. On. It." 0-3 commanded.

"Lay...on it?" Eop asked, not sure what that meant.

"Place. Your. Back. On. It."

"Oh, that is what you mean. Okay." Eop lied on the structure, and 0-3 proceeded to inspect him for any injuries. 0-3 then walked over to one of the drawers on the left.

"What are you going to do with Lee-Der?" Eop's voice grew concerned.

"That. Beast. He. Is. Just. Like. The. Rest. Of. His. Ethite. Kind. Will. Be. Imprisoned. Indefinitely." 0-3 explained.

"On what charges? He...he did not hurt anybody." Eop defended his friend.

"He. Resisted. Arrest." 0-3 argued.

"Only because he did not understand his crimes."

"His. Crime. Was. Existing. Bring. A. Glitch." 0-3 explained.

"So that is what you are, some kind of task force to stop..."Glitches?" Eop stated but was confused still.

"Precisely." 0-3 said. "We. Were. Made. By. The. Developers. To. Stop. Glitches. Living. In. Programs. That. Negatively. Influence. Video. Games."

"Ah, so The Developers created-" Eop was interrupted.

"How. Is. He." 0-1 said. He had walked into the room without making a sound.

0-3 turned to look at 0-1, "He. Is. In. Perfect. Condition. To. Be. Sent. Back."

"Sent back? By myself? I will never be able to play Ping-Pong again...my game will become obsolete!"

0-3 thought on Eop's words for a moment, then spoke, "He. Has. A. Point."

"I...suppose. You. Are. Right." 0-1 reluctantly admitted. "But. We. Cannot. Just. Let. Him. Stay."

"I could become a Game Protector!" Eop shouted out quickly.

0-3 and 0-1 looked at one another, "He. Does. Have. The. Physique." 0-3 said.

"I. Will. Get. The. Other's. Opinions. Though. I. Honor. Your. Willingness. Eop. I. See. Good. In. You." 0-1 said, walking away.

"Do you think they will let me?" Eop asked.

"I. Believe. So." 0-3 stated.

Eop had been checked and as believed, had no injuries. With the inspection over with, 0-1 ushered Eop over to discuss the idea of him joining them.

"I. Have. Talked. With. The. Others," 0-1 began. "They. Are. All. Willing. To. Give. You. A. Chance."

"Thank you. I promise that I will try my best not to burden any of you," Eop reassured him.

"Tomorrow. Your. Training. Will. Begin," 0-1 paused. "However. I. Must. Reveal. Something. To. You. Ensure. This. Path. Is. Truly. One. You. Want. To. Follow."

Eop nodded.

They proceeded to walk to a room with a book on a pedestal. This room was not like the others. It was in the shape of a dome, and it shined color, a golden color. On the roof hung a lantern, which brightened the pedestal, and reflected off the book.

"What is that?" Eop asked.

"The. Prophecy. What. You. Are. To. Believe." 0-1 explained.

0-1 did not speak for another few moments.

"When. The. Developers. Created. Us. They. Encoded. A. Prophecy. Into. Our. Minds. They. Also. Planted. It. Here. In. This. Book," 0-1 explained. "Go. Ahead. Read. It. As. I. Speak."

Eop raced over to the book, eager to uncover the answers to all the questions he yearned to understand.

"We. Believe. That. The. Developers. Will. One. Day. Send. A. Prophet. And. He. Shall. Unite. Us. With. Paradise. Separate. Us. From. The. Glitches." 0-1 continued.

"Separate? It says here that the Prophet will unite Glitches and Game Protectors alike; in paradise," Eop questioned.

"A. Simple. Misunderstanding. The. Book. May. Sound. As. If.

That. Is. What. It. Means. But. It. Is. False."

"Oh..." Eop still did not understand, but he did not want to push 0-1.

"We. Will. Know. Of. The. Prophet's. Identity. For. He. Will. Do. A. Many. Great. Miracles."

"A man shall yield to the prophet in battle." Eop mumbled under his breath, "The prophet shall calm a fire." "The Prophet will turn golden a room." "The prophet shall disarm an army." "The prophet shall heal a...Lectin." "What is...a Lectin?" Eop asked.

"A. Man. Or. Woman. With. Red. Tinted. Eyes. A. Demon. In. Bodily. Form." 0-1 explained.

"Interesting," Eop replied.

"Are. You. Willing. To. Believe. In. This. Prophecy. And. Become. A. Game. Protector?" 0-1 questioned. "Yes. It intrigues me. I want to learn more. Learn your ways." Eop said.

"It. Is. Settled. Then. Welcome. Eop." 0-1 said.

Eop smiled.

"First. You. Cross. Your. Arms. Near. Your. Chest. Like. This. Your. Arms. Should. Be. In. The. Shape. Of. The. Letter. "X" As. the. Humans. Call. It." 0-1 taught Eop.

"Like this?" Eop asked after doing as told.

"Precisely," 0-1 responded. "Now. Extend. Your. Right. Index. Finger. And. Arch. It. Slightly. Then. Extend. Out. Your. Thumb."

"Keep the thumb straight?" Eop asked.

"Yes." O-1 answered.

29

"Okay." Eop widened his stance and breathed in then out. He then crossed his arms, extended and bent his index finger, and finally extended out his thumb.

0-1 nodded in approval, "Now. Say. Two. Enemies. Were. To. Strike. You. What. Move. Will. You. Perform. To. Counter. The. Attack?"

"I would swing my right arm out like this, keeping my thumb and index finger in the same position." Eop explained as he did the actions at the same time.

"That. Is. Correct. Your. Index. Finger. And. Thumb. Or. The. Backside. Of. Your. Hand. Would. Block. The. Incoming. Enemy. Attack." 0-1 continued, "From. This. Position. You. Would. Swing. Your. Left. Arm. Out. And. Strike. The. Second. Enemy."

Eop performed the actions 0-1 had just taught him, and then responded:

"I understand," Eop said as he nodded slowly.

"This. Second. Variation. Of. The. Attack. Can. Be. Performed. If. There. Is. Only. One. Enemy." 0-1 paused to allow his words to meditate in Eop's mind. "You. First. Perform. Almost. Everything. I. Have. Just. Taught. You. But. This. Time. Swing. Your. Left. Arm. Back. And. Then. To. The. Right."

Eop performed this version of the attack, and as he did it, he asked: "What is this attack, and it's variation called?"

"The. Attack. Itself. Is. Called. The. Double. Additional. Block. And. It's. Variation. Is. Called. The. Singular. Secular. Block." 0-1 responded.

"Mmmm," Eop responded with intrigue.

The Training of Eop, August 8, 1974-August 7, 1975

Eop continued to train, learning more melee and range attack skills. In addition, he learned how to use daggers, swords, and range weapons such as Jillits—which are like bows and arrows, but with a fuse at the end of the arrow. Once the arrow fuse catches fire, it takes a few moments to go off, and shoot. This weapon is used from quite a long range, used to start ambushes.

Eop mastered the "Swift Dagger Strike," a move which is simply using a dagger in quick—and careful—precision, along the most vital parts of an enemy's code.

Eop learned how to "Reaction Focus," the ability to be so self-aware and in tune with your surroundings that almost every attack is instinctively dodged.

Most importantly, Eop learned the "Head-strike." This move was a counterattack that could be performed when an enemy flew a fist toward their opponent's head. If you were being struck, you would simply evade the fist, grab the enemy's arm if possible, and then—with all your might—use your head to stun the enemy by hitting their face.

With all these skills achieved, and many more to mention, Eop slowly, but surely, proved himself; and was ready to become a Game Protector.

Eop's Formal Induction, August 7, 1975

With his training completed, Eop found peace within himself, a peace he had not had in a long time.

"Eop." 0-1 called out one day, standing behind Eop, who had been studying the Armor of the Great. "You. Have. Been. Staring. At. That. Armor. For. A. Long. Time," 0-1 continued.

"It. Would. Look. Good. On. You," 0-1 finished.

"Why do you speak like that?" Eop asked, turning around to face 0-1, unknowingly about to change things. "Like. What?" 0-1 asked, unaware of the pauses in his, and the other Game Protectors, speech.

"Like that!" Eop exclaimed eagerly, "I apologize for my rudeness, but this question has been sticking in my mind for quite some time: You have pauses in between each word, why?" Eop asked with haste, truly wanting the answer to his inquiry.

"I-was...not. Aware. Of-of that." 0-1 struggled to say, realizing what Eop had said is true, and trying to correct it. "Do. The-" 0-1 paused, closing his eyes, and wrinkling his face, yet against struggling to say what he wanted to say normally: "Do the other. Game Protectors...struggle with. This?" 0-1 continued, barely able to get his words out this way.

"I am afraid so," Eop reluctantly admitted, trying not to offend 0-1.

"That is....quite. Interesting. I never. Noticed it." 0-1 paused, scrunching his face, and then sighing: "Forgive...me. Eop. This new speech...pattern. It is difficult to learn." 0-1 apologized. Eop began chuckling.

"No need for apologies my friend! Come, let us walk," Eop said in a welcoming and friendly voice, as he walked over to 0-1, and put his hand on his shoulder.

"I must ask. What is it you came to me for?" Eop asked with intrigue, but already knew the answer.

"Come...walk...with...me. I...will explain," 0-1 instructed, and

Eop followed 0-1 down the hall, full of enthusiasm.

"I Have. An. Idea. But I. Need. To. Talk To. The. Other. Game Protectors. First," 0-1 admitted, his speech somewhat improving.

Eop jumped with excitement, "I am curious…and excited. What do you have in mind?"

0-1 let out a chuckle, but quickly his face turned curious and confused, since he had never experienced emotions—laughter, or chuckling—before. 0-1 turned his head, looking to the corner of the ceiling and thinking.

"How did that happen?" 0-1 wondered in his mind. *Has Eop finally rubbed off on me? It would appear so.*

When Eop and 0-1 arrived at the Grand Hall, The Game Protectors were sitting down, discussing something in whispers. Upon seeing Eop and 0-1, every Game Protector stood up and bowed their heads at Eop and 0-1. In unison, they said in a monotone voice: "Commander."

"Greetings! I have decided that. Eop of Ping-Pong is...ready to. Officially join our ranks!" 0-1 stated and exclaimed, "Ah ha! I have figured it out!" 0-1 said cheerfully.

"Figured. What. Out?" 0-3 asked.

"Eop informed me that we have been talking oddly. We pause after each word." 0-1 explained and then paused, "However, we can work on that later, right now..." 0-1 paused again, putting his left hand on Eop's shoulder, and looking at him. Eop proceeded to look back at 0–1. "We congratulate and honor our new member! Cheers to you, brother!" 0-1 yet again exclaimed. The Game Protectors then raised their glasses to Eop.

Eop smiled. "I also have an idea for all of you. Having names, names like mine!" Eop thought out loud.

"Not. A. Bad. Idea., Eop." 0-1 said, "I. Would. Like. Mine. To. Be. Lead."

"Mine. Would. Be. Dawn." 0-3 said.

"Mine. Instilla." 0-5 said.

"Protect." 0-2 said.

"I. Am. Thinking. Upside." 0-4 stated.

"Vice." 0-6 said.

"Hybrid." 0-7 said.

After this, Eop put the Armor of the Great on. This armor had a black bodysuit and orange armor plating.

Eop's First Mission, Crafting, October 8, 1975

The surrounding area was grassy, and a medium green color. On the grass stood an army of Glitches, signs in their hands; protesting.

The portal of The Game Protectors opened, and they came soaring down, landing on the ground harshly.

"Surrender, you dirty Ethite scums!" Lead yelled.

"Please do not hurt us!" Settings, a Glitch, echoed in terror, "We are only protesting!"

"Against The Humans? Against The Developers? Heresy!"

The Game Protectors followed behind Lead as he charged at The Glitches. Some Glitches ran, others stood their ground, resisting.

Eop chased after one of the fleeing Glitches, Settings, and managed to pin him to the ground with a knife to his throat.

"Why are you doing these evil deeds?" Eop asked.

"Evil?" Settings struggled to chuckle, "They have brainwashed you!"

"How so?" Eop asked,

"You are renovating this land, renovating my home! You and all your false creators have you here to exterminate us, and start production on a new video game," Settings argued.

"The prophecy, and The Developers are true!" Eop argued.

"What reason do you have to believe that? Or any of the rubbish

The Game Protectors spew? How many times have they altered or contradicted their own book?" Settings contained, "Think on that."

The other Game Protectors continued fighting and chasing the other Glitches, eventually catching and arresting them all.

Lead, with a Glitch beside him, then ushered Eop to follow them through a new portal, back to Watch Base 01.

"Who is that Glitch?" Eop asked Lead.

"Nobody important," Lead said.

"My name is Tacitus! I have done no wrong!" Tacitus argued.

Eop tightly gripped Settings by the arm, taking him with him. They all then returned to Watch Base 01, where The Glitches were put into holding cells.

Lee-Der Plotting His Escape, Watch Base 01, October 9, 1975

The cell Lee-Der was housed in was the eighth of twenty on the left. The cell was designed for Glitches that were smaller than the rest. As for the actual exterior and interior, it was not easy on the eyes. Unlike the rest of Watch Base 01, these cells were not made of the richest materials around. The Game Protectors instead, designed the cells out of purple and black checkered textures that covered the walls. As for the floor, it too, was made out of a checkered pattern, but instead of purple and black, the ground was yellow and black.

Across the hall, Lee-Der could hear the Game Protector Instilla talking with one of The Glitches, Tacitus, though, Instilla did not notice it. Once Instilla left, Lee-Der let his anger begin to take control.

Lee-Der had his eyes closed and was facing the back wall of his cell. Lee-Der drove his fist into the ground, both angrily and firmly. "This is not fair!" his voice shaking the entire room with agitation.

"Silence yourself, Lee-Der!" a Glitch snarled. The Glitch that had spoken up was Settings. He was found in a cell that prohibited him from using his abilities. All this time, Settings was the most powerful Glitch. The Game Protectors had faced the possibility that Lee-Der would later change that.

Settings sighed, "I am sorry." Settings admitted, "I usually control my anger, but in times like these, when our kind are threatened so-" Settings couldn't find the word to complete his sentence,

"Poorly?" Lee-Der replied, tilting his head to state his word.

"Yes, poorly," Settings agreed, his voice now calm and stoic.

Lee-Der turned around, to face the Glitch he was talking with, "I do in fact know you," Lee-Der said after taking a glance at Settings.

"Before you ask how I know, I have overheard the speeches of The Game Protectors. They said that you are scrawny, but powerful, influential, and dangerous."

Lee-Der chuckled, remarking on the stupidity of The Game Protectors. Settings followed in suit. "I am no danger," Settings remarked, his words barely coming out through his laughter. "I simply want Glitches and Game Protectors to live peaceful lives together," Settings concluded, alongside with his laugh.

"A wise dream," Lee-Der smiled, "But a naive one." Lee-Der's face drooped with sadness and depression.

"It is possible!" Settings argued passionately.

"Not without much bloodshed," Lee-Der remarked, making Settings realize he had no argument to stand on.

The two sat in silence for a moment. "What does one cynic like you believe then?" Settings asked, his tone coming across somewhat rude.

"I am no cynic. I just see this situation for what it truly is," Lee-Der defended. "It will be many years before The Game Protectors discover that not every Glitch is intentionally a problem. Until then, until equality presents itself, we must escape here. We cannot just allow ourselves to be wrongfully incarcerated, especially when most of us haven't done anything wrong," Lee-Der paused, and tilted his head to think. "We shall find ourselves in The Borderlands of The Superworld. That will be our home. Eventually, The Game Protectors will find us. We will fight to protect our land. For many years, we will have to fight them when they come. However, I do believe that won't be how it will be for eternity. I promise you that. I believe one day there will be a Game Protector that comes that will offer us peace," Lee-Der said, not only inspiring Settings, but inspiring many other imprisoned Glitches too.

"They will not win," one Glitch screamed.

"Me too, I would never let another Game Protector steal my land from me!" another Glitch boasted.

Settings looked around at all the commotion that was beginning to arise, even shook his head in agreement, and smiled. "I suppose I'm in," Settings decided.

"Enough! No more one-by-ones! If you agree, say Noream!" Lee-Der commanded.

"Noream!"

The word flooded the entire jail block.

Lee-Der's Escape, Watch Base 01, October 11, 1975

"You are honestly going to keep me here for eternity? We were friends for goodness sakes!" Lee-Der said to Eop one day, as Eop had been walking past the cells. Eop stopped in his tracks abruptly and closed his eyes. He was trying to avoid Lee-Der's temptations and keep his composure. He then continued walking, but after a few steps, his curiosity ended up getting the better of him.

"The Game Protectors say that you are a threat, and as long as you and The Glitches exist-" Eop turned to face Lee-Der, and think on his next words, "We and The Playable Characters will never truly be safe," Eop argued.

"And do their words find any merit with you?" Lee-Der persisted.

Eop thought for a moment, walking over to Lee-Der's cell, noticing Instilla talking with one of The Glitches, Tacitus.

"What are you doing?" Eop asked Instilla.

"Oh! I am just interrogating this...Ethite," she said unconvincingly, but Eop shrugged.

Eop then stood in front of the long, thick gray bars. Eop reached out his hand and grabbed the bar like he was choking it. Without Eop noticing, Instilla had walked off.

"I do not know." Eop admitted in a muddled and mumbled voice. "I have seen Glitches to be evil, horrid creatures." Eop praised, "but I have also seen Glitches like you... who are yet to do anything wrong," Eop explained.

"It is true, that some Glitches are truly evil. But are you going to listen to The Game Protectors' dogma? Are you really going to believe that every Glitch is inherently evil?" Lee-Der asked almost as if his question was rhetorical.

Eop stared deeply into Lee-Der's eyes. They were pure black, mesmerizing and attractive. It was almost as if they were gigantic magnets. Lee-Der's expression was one of relentlessness, tiredness, longing to be free. If you were to see it, you would almost feel bad for him even if you didn't take a liking to Glitches.

Eop contemplated Lee-Der's words with immense thoughts, and complexity.

"You deserve freedom, my friend," Eop said reluctantly, almost as if he weren't sure if he were doing the right thing. He then proceeded to slowly grab the key out of his belt, and then held it in the palm of his hand. He looked at the key. Like it was a magnificent art piece, and then he decided to put it in the lock and turn it.

Lee-Der and The Glitches Escape, October 11, 1975

Lee-Der methodically walked out of his cell, each footstep as light as a drizzle of rain. He then secretly took Eop's keys to the cell.

Lee-Der looked at Eop longingly, carefully.

"Thank you, brother," Lee-Der said under his breath and

proceeded to walk off. Eop looked to his feet, thinking. He then heard the whistling of keys, and the eerie echoes of a turning lock. He jolted his head towards the sound, something almost giving himself whiplash.

"Lee-Der! Do not-" It was too late. Lee-Der had opened Settings' cell. In a rapid instant, Settings walked out of his cell, his smirk as sharp as a blade. With one hand motion, he sent Eop flying backward, with the fingers on his right hand plunged deeply into the right side of Eop's face like tiny daggers. Eop slid across the ground, tearing the programming on his back clean off. Eop laid on the ground for a moment, recollecting his thoughts. He then sat up and attempted to pull his fingers out from his skin. He dragged his fingers down his face, his skin ripping like paper sunk in water. Painfully, he drove his fingers out of his face, and violently moved his hand away from his body.

His right side of his face was left with a scar of a dark-grayish-black color. Three-line marks were written from his forehead, and ended at his neck, where he finally ripped his fingers abruptly out of his chin. Eop moaned in excruciating pain. Lee-Der's face turned a devilish red. Without a thought, he raised Settings high above the ground, "Look what you did to him! He freed us you fool! He was my friend!" Lee-Der restrained Settings with the force of a solid wall.

"And he...is inclined to do the opposite!" Settings argued with struggle, "He will not!" Lee-Der threw Settings down onto the ground. "Free the rest of them," Lee-Der commanded angrily.

Settings raised his left arm and curved his fingers. Suddenly, a ruckus of metal bending and rusting away filled the room.

Suddenly, a mob of furry-filled Glitches busted out of their cells and overpopulated the hallway. They all rushed out behind Lee-Der.

The Attack on Watch Base 01, October 11, 1975

"We have a breech!" A voice yelled out, "Sound the bell!" The voice came closer, "Eop! Eop! Are you okay?"

Eop opened his eyes slightly and squinted.

"Lead! Lead, is that you?" Eop asked in a faint voice.

"Yes Eop. It is me." Lead responded. "Here, let me assist you up."

Lead proceeded to grab Eop's arm and lift him up. Eop could barely stand. "I got you, Eop." Lead put Eop's arm over his shoulder, and he grabbed his waist. They then took tiny steps toward the hallway exit. "What happened, Eop?" Lead asked.

Eop sighed in both pain and reluctance. "In truth…it was…my fault. Eop struggled to breathe, "Lee-Der manipulated me. He tricked me into thinking he was unjustly imprisoned," Lead and Eop stopped walking.

Lead's face turned to the color of a setting sun.

"We will discuss this later," Lead growled.

Inch by inch they made it closer to the exit of the hallway. Screams, roars, and other destructive sounds could be heard. Swords clashing, teeth grinding. Tripping, bumping. It was clear Watch Base 01 was being ripped apart, piece by piece, noise by noise.

Finally, Lead and Eop made it to the door that led into the main room.

Gently and carefully Lead laid Eop on the ground, a little further past the left door. Eop leaned against the silver metal pole of a jail cell, feeling the cold embrace. He coughed.

"You are in no position to fight, Eop," Lead said as he continuously shifted his vision. He looked at the double doors, and then at Eop, and then at the doors again. "Remain here, once you hear no sound, come into the main room. Stay safe," Lead commanded.

Lead then slid closer to the double doors, to the point where they could feel his breath. He then tilted his head down slowly, sighed, and kicked the doors open.

Eop closed his eyes loosely and flinched as the double doors shut loudly across from him.

The Demotion of Eop, October 11, 1975

After an hour or so, the sound of battle subsided. Battle cries were no longer shouted, and weapons no longer clashed upon one another. Eop gently opened his eyes. He sighed of both relief and uncertainty. What would The Game Protectors do with him? How would they react to what he did?

Suddenly the double doors jolted open like a demon Eop was afraid of facing.

"Eop!" Lead shouted.

"Over...over here sir." Eop stated faintly under his breath, like a child who knew he had done something bad and was about to be punished by his parents.

Lead turned to face Eop.

With no words, Lead ushered Eop to rise up with a simple motion of his hand. Lead then walked back into the main room, and Eop reluctantly followed him.

Eop looked at The Game Protectors. They were cleaning up the main room, picking up fragments of broken furniture, and putting their weaponry back into safe keeping.

"Tell them what you have done, Eop," Lead said menacingly.

Eop sighed, and The Game Protectors fixed their gaze upon him.

"I freed Lee-Der, who then freed The Glitches," Eop admitted.

The room exploded into an outburst of scolding and mangled voices; indistinguishable to tell which voice was which.

"But you have to understand!" Eop defended himself, "Some of these Glitches are not bad!"

"They poison video games! They ruin the immersion experience for The Humans!" Dawn argued.

"They do not intend to do so! They cannot help the way they were born!" Eop continued.

"They are nothing but animals, Eop. They are not capable of emotions-of. Of the intelligence we possess," Upside said.

"Neither were you!" Eop paused, "I joined when? One...two years ago? Before then you all were nothing but a program a...a steel rod of a person. I mean not to insult you, but-Jain! The Glitches are real...more authentic than any of you will probably ever be!"

The Game Protectors gasped.

"That is enough!" Lead stomped his foot, "You are a remarkable soldier Eop, and full of potential. You have come too far to simply be discarded or exiled, however I believe you are not worthy of the rank you currently possess. Therefore...I shall take it from you," Lead stated.

Eop stepped back and scoffed, "I understand what I have done, but is this not too extreme?" Eop asked in disillusionment.

"Extreme!" Lead yelled in anger, not only did you assist our enemies, but you also defended them!" Lead screamed and then paused, "Let me put it this way, Eop. It is quite generous that I spare you; let alone give you an opportunity to regain your rank, after what you have done."

"What of The Glitches, Commander?" Upside decided to ask.

Lead turned around to face Upside, keeping his gaze of disappointment fixed on Eop as he turned. "I suspect they will run to The Borderlands," Lead answered.

"We should go after them while they are still close!" Upside encouraged.

"That would be suicide! The extinction of our race!" Lead shook his head, "No." He paused, "Every year or so we shall send a team over to The Borderlands in attempt to recapture those Ethites," Lead suggested.

"Team?" Eop said out loud in confusion, "What team? There is seven of-"

"Six. Six of us," Vice corrected Eop.

Eop rocked back in confusion and shock: "What of Instilla? Did she-" Eop hoped his thoughts were incorrect.

"We do not know," Lead regretfully admitted.

"She went after some Glitch named Tacitus," Protect revealed.

Eop nodded, "I remember him. I remember...you arresting him." Eop grew disappointed with his actions. Silence followed for a few moments.

"Anyway," Lead moved on, "To answer your question Eop; not that you deserve to know, but...times are changing," Lead begun, "The Developers never anticipated that The Glitches would escape...and neither did we. That is why there are so few of us. We were designed to simply go in and stop threats, and then return here; until the day where we would live in peace: no longer needed."

"But there was always a backup plan," Eop realized.

"Precisely. We will pray to The Developers to create more of us," Lead stated with a hopeful expression.

Chapter 1...
JUMPER ORIGINS

The Introduction of Jumper, February 2, 1981

Seeing as though they weren't able to be married in Watch Base 01, Tacitus and Instilla eloped to The Borderlands, a region of The Superworld, in order to get married. They then looked for a place to live and eventually found an acre of land in the middle of the center of the Upper Left Side, on the edge of The Borderlands region.

Though she returned to work with The Game Protectors, Instilla kept her relationship with Tacitus secret; and protected Tacitus from the Game Protector's year-after-year searches for the escaped Glitches.

As time passed, Watch Base 01 grew from a simple military base to the capital city of The Superworld. Tall, glistening and reflective business buildings were built, small markets were squeezed into the smallest of crevices and corners; and most of all the population grew from a mere seven Game Protectors, to over ten-thousand and counting. This created the first generation, the Elder Game Protectors—the original seven, and future generations.

As for Superworld itself, The Developers continued to work on it slowly turning it into a video game.

Rules changed as well. Even though he was shunned and thought to be a betrayer of the Game Protector cause, Eop of Ping-Pong's influence remained in the land.

Eop made it so that even Glitches could find residence in the city; however, most Glitches who lived in Watch Base 01 were poorer than most.

They were often homeless, or lacked sufficient income, since most employers denied The Glitches of even the simplest of jobs.

To make matters worse, most Game Protectors still despised The Glitches, especially the Elders. It is a mere miracle that Eop could even convince them to allow Glitches into the city!

If a Glitch took one simple step onto the pavement of Watch Base 01, all would tilt their heads, and immediately mock and throw insults at the Glitch.

This...was the world Jumper was born into.

But who was Jumper?

He was the son of Tacitus and Instilla—a Glitch, and a Game Protector—making him...a Half-code. The perfect candidate to fix all of this, to unite The Glitches and The Game Protectors, to be...the Prophet.

Introduction of Jumper November 27, 1995

His tightly knit, golden hair, breezed in the whispering wind. It made him appear as if there was a pot of gold upon his head. His gigantic striking blue eyes reflected a thousand flickering lanterns, in a vibrant gray and His face was gentle, and as soft as a smooth, light gray stone: patiently waiting.

His clothing laid loose on his body, blowing in the wind. A multitude of minuscule rips and cuts polluted both his shirt and pants, like a deadly plague.

He sat barefoot on the warm green grass; his toes slightly grabbing the stalks and feeling the morning dew in between them.

Muffled were the sounds of the townsfolk speaking, and then...boots? Jumper heard boots crashing down in the grass behind him. Almost naturally, Jumper turned to look, and there was his father.

"Jumper?" Tacitus called out.

"Yes Father?" Jumper replied.

"I have business to attend to, and your mother is out on duty. I need you to go to the market and retrieve some items for me."

"Retrieve items from the market!" Jumper jumped up with joy, smiling with paper-colored teeth.

"Now Jumper," Tacitus raised his open palm.

"Ooh, I promise I will not cause any trouble, Father! I will be careful!"

Tacitus chuckled, and smiled widely, "Ok, I trust you."

Jumper immediately dashed off, but then heard his father calling out to him again, "Forgetting something, son?"

"Oh! I never got the list!" Jumper mumbled under his breath, as he turned and ran back around.

Tacitus had the list in his palm, and as Jumper tried to grab it: "Here..." Tacitus playfully moved his arm out of Jumper's reach.

"Give it here!" Jumper said spiritedly, smiling as he hopped around, trying to get the list.

"You go," Tacitus gave Jumper the list.

Jumper laughed with joy, "I love you, Father."

"Come here," Tacitus asked. Jumper did so, and the father and son hugged.

They then took a step back from one another: "See you again soon, son," Tacitus bid him farewell.

"See you again soon!" Jumper exclaimed as he ran off.

Jumper in the Market, November 27, 1995

He ran as the speed of light, his hair fluttering in with the wind. Gently, the wind lightly breezed past Jumper, a similar feeling to touching water.

His arms followed loosely behind him, floating, like two bubbles. His feet stomped into the ground causing spots of rectangular craters.

From a mile away, you could hear Jumper's rushing feet; see his shadow reflect off the buildings, and on the sunlit floor.

Citizens looked at Jumper with dislike, with hatred. Not only was he an Ethite Glitch, but he was a Half-code as well.

Respectfully, Jumper slowed, and carefully weaved his way through the crowded streets.

Whilst walking, those who saw Jumper threw insults at him, mocked him, called him a no good Ethite. Jumper did not respond to any of these insults.

Eventually, Jumper arrived at The Marketplace of Watch Base 01 and walked up to one of the booth-stands.

"You are not from this land, are you?" Ballied, the salesman, asked Jumper.

Jumper looked up at him, still catching his breath from running. "I apologize sir, I did not hear you. What did you say?"

"You are an Ethite," Ballied replied with anger, "I do not do business with Ethites."

"Please sir, my father needs some items from the market. It will only take a moment! I have all the money!" Jumper begged.

"I. Do. Not. Do. Business. With. Ethites." Ballied restated.

It almost felt as if the entire marketplace stopped and grew silent. Jumper closed his eyes and opened them.

"Woe to you o' Ballied, who judges others. Whom Judges Glitches! If you continue trotting this path, defying the prophecy, you will not inherit paradise," Jumper said, sending Ballied back with fear.

Ballied did not say a word. He took Jumper's list and put the items from it into a basket.

Jumper took the basket and left.

"How did he know...my name?" Ballied asked in fear, almost to himself.

"I do not know. That kid is...weird. I have heard some rumors that he is Tacitus and Instilla's son," a customer replied.

"Really? If so...I could win a reward, maybe even a position in the center of Watch Base 01!" Ballied grew in excitement, "Maybe...I will let The Game Protectors know of this exchange. Of this...kid."

The Arrest of Tacitus, November 27, 1995

As Jumper skipped home excitedly, his face had a wholesome grin; unaware of The Game Protectors following him home. With the wooden basket of items tightly gripped by its handle, Jumper breezed his way through the crowded streets, maneuvering through many obstacles that came through his way.

Jumper also remained polite, saying such phrases as "Excuse me!" and "Pardon me!" Whenever he required to get past somebody. The crowd on the other hand, remained rude. Those who caught a glimpse of Jumper almost instinctually yelled:

"Ethite!" Or "Glitch!" And to those who noticed Jumper as a Half-code, well...that is exactly what they screamed: "Half-code!"

However, Jumper ignored their insults, and he continued on his way.

As he grew closer to home, the fragrance of his mother's perfume flooded his nostrils. He grew joyful to see her.

However, Jumper smelled something else, something...foreign it seemed. Then he heard it.

"Get off of me!" Tacitus growled.

Jumper sprinted towards his father immediately. Once he was mere meters away from him, Jumper saw guards, Game Protectors. Jumper glanced around for a spot to hide, and luckily, he saw a log. He walked over to it silently, crouched down, and hid, slightly peeking his head out.

"We have been looking for you for a long time, Tacitus," one of The Game Protectors taunted.

"I never did anything wrong! The Elder Game Protectors arrested me simply for existing!" Tacitus defended himself trying to fight back.

"Then what about your escape from custody. Is that not a crime in which you broke?" The Game Protector argued.

Tacitus turned silent and stopped fighting.

"That is what I thought, Ethite."

Another Game Protector came behind Tacitus, kicking his legs out and sending him to his knees. Tacitus groaned and lowered his head.

"Rumors also say that you have had an affair with one of our own. Who was it? Instilla? Some even say...you had a Half-code son. Now that is a crime, is it not?" The Game Protector from before mocked.

Instilla busted out of the back door of their house, "What is going on?" she yelled in anger.

"They are arresting me! Just like before!" Tacitus exclaimed.

"And what of me?" Instilla argued, "Why not arrest me to? For I have broken the law as well."

The Game Protector busted into heavy laughter, "Break the Law? You should know that Elder Game Protectors—such as yourself—cannot break the law! Come on squadron, let us leave from this stupidity-filled acre of filth."

The Game Protectors left, taking Tacitus away. He no longer fought.

"Goodbye, my love," Tacitus echoed in the wind.

Silently, Jumper crept out from the log he had hid behind. His mother, who had been weeping hysterically, heard him. She turned her head, and looked at Jumper as if her heart had sunk.

"Oh darling," she wrapped Jumper in a hug, and closed her eyes, "How long were you here?" Her voice trembled, as she extended Jumper away, kneeling down to see his face.

"I heard almost all of it," Jumper collected himself. "What are they going to do to dad?"

"Oh honey, nothing is going to happen. I promise this will all be sorted out," Jumper's mother attempted to reassure him, but even she remained doubtful of her words.

The Sentence of Tacitus, Grand Judgment Court, November 30, 1995

"Tacitus." The Judge, Ovalrod, stated loudly and firmly. He almost had a sense of anger in his tone. Ovalrod paused, "You are hereby condemned of heinous actions by this court."

Jumper and his mother, Instilla, were consumed with shock, "You were aware that having relations with a Game Protector is no less illegal for your kind," Ovalrod continued. Jumper's father looked at the judge with a disgusted expression, "My kind?" Tacitus mumbled furiously under his breath, "Pardon?" The Judge exclaimed. Tacitus said nothing in reply; instead, he turned around and looked to Jumper and Instilla with sorrow. The guards then forced Tacitus back around, making him reluctantly glance at the Judge.

"I sentence you to four-quadrilaterals in Nomadin Avery," the Judge concluded. Half of the courtroom mocked and laughed at Jumper's father, and the other half, the half that Jumper and his mother were on, gasped. Nomadin Avery at this time, was not the most secure prison, but rather the poorest prison. It was a sure fact that if you attained a sickness in this prison, you would not be given the correct care, and that illness would most likely lead to an early grave.

Jumper's father was ushered away by the guards and taken into a Processing Room.

Jumper...never saw his father again.

"Any objections to the ruling shall no longer be accepted at this time," Ovalrod stated chillingly, the words echoing in Jumper's mind.

Jumper Becomes a Game Protector, Watch Base 01's Induction Room, November 30, 1999

On this day, an unrecognizable young man had come to Watch Base 01. He had dark blond hair, unsaturated green eyes, and light-gray skin tone. The man was wearing a brownish-dark-gray shirt, coupled with black pants, which both were stained with some brown color. It was clear the young man was poor, especially since his clothing also had very visible holes in them. The young man proceeded to walk up to and open the front door of Watch Base 01. He walked his way to the Induction Room, being stared at by the many visitors that had come to Watch Base 01 that day. These glances were ones of judgment, as The Game Protectors mocked both the young man's clothing, and what he looked like. Eventually, the young man got past these halls, and into the Induction Room. The Induction Room was crowded, and full of lengthy waiting lines. The young man went over to line three and waited there for a considerable amount of time. Two hours to be exact. Once the young man arrived at the front of the line, he spoke with the Inductor, Ballied. Ballied looked at the man, glancing up to the man's head, all the way to his feet. He too was judging him. Ballied chuckled.

"So, you're here t' become a-uh...Game Protector?" Ballied asked the young man, as he continued to chuckle.

"Yes. I want to change things. End this...this feud between Game Protectors and Glitches." The young man revealed, his voice full of eagerness, and excitement.

Ballied almost died of laughter, "A...great. Dream. Boy," Ballied struggled to say, continuously laughing. Ballied breathed in, gaining composure. "But who are you, to think such...impossible dreams?" Ballied said.

"Jumper." The man answered in a friendly manner, smiling.

Ballied stood back, his face showing a haunted and surprised look. Those who were still in the Induction Room gasped, and some even covered their mouths with their hands.

Jumper laughed and shook his head. Jumper then looked directly into the eyes of Ballied.

"No need to be afraid of me, Ballied. I forgive you for what you did to my father," Jumper said in a calm nice voice, soothing face, yet again smiling. Jumper turned around facing all of those who gasped at him: "In fact, none of you have to worry about me, for I promise not to harm you, for I forgive all of the insults thrown at my face," Jumper promised, again trying to be friendly.

"I promise to always be kind to you! To not allow my emotions and thoughts to have a misinterpretation of you! To be a friend you need, a reliable source! I intend to deliver you! To unite you with The Glitches, to harmonize you and them!" Jumper exclaimed with happiness and excitement.

"I will not let you do that, you half-Glitch-wannabe Game Protector," Ballied said.

He room cheered him on.

"Please, Ballied," Jumper pleaded.

Ballied shook his head.

"Get your wonderful Ethite-self outta here," Ballied's tone grew frustrated.

Jumper walked off and the room erupted into furry-filled insults and rude remarks towards Jumper. Ballied tried calming the room.

Jumper was right about to leave, having his hand tightly gripping the door handle, but then he stopped.

Jumper shut his eyes, and immediately the door began turning a royal yellow color.

The Game Protectors were in awe, and Ballied grew terrified. Jumper then let go of the door handle, turned around, and walked over to Ballied; with each step Jumper took, the walls and floor turned golden.

Ballied, without hesitation, gave Jumper a room number on a sheet of paper, and Jumper walked off. The room then slowly turned back to its original color.

Chapter 2...
FRIENDS OR FOES?

Jumper Meets Who Would Become His First Followers, November 30, 1999

Jumper knocked firmly on the door to his new quarters. Jumper waited a moment, nobody answered. Jumper examined the door he was standing in front of, trying to make sure he was in the right place. This door was brown with a golden handle in the middle. This door also had a black plate with golden lining around the edges. This plate displayed the room number: 0310. Jumper was in the right place, and so, he knocked again.

The door was opened reluctantly by Bolder, the man who would become Jumper's closest friend. Bolder wore a green helmet which had the letter "B" in the middle of it. This helmet also had a green mouth guard which connected to the sides of Bolder's helmet by two rectangular green pieces on both sides. This mouth guard also had dark-gray lines in the middle, on the ends, and near Bolder's cheeks. Bolder also wore a dark-blue chest piece with a green outline, and no collar. He had a dark-grey bodysuit under his armor. Lastly, Bolder wore armored green gloves, and armored green boots.

"Why. Hello. I. Am. Bolder. How. Can. I. Assist. You?" Bolder asked in a serious and yet calm voice. It was clear he lacked emotion. He spoke like the first-generation Game Protectors.

Jumper smiled with eagerness, "Hello! I am Jumper. I am here to become a Game Protector, and I was given space in this room to rest." Jumper extended out his arm to Bolder, insisting on a handshake.

Bolder looked at Jumper, and then at his arm. Bolder clicked his tongue. He then tilted his head, and quickly repositioned it. He was thinking. He then slowly raised his arm to shake Jumper's hand. They proceeded to shake hands.

"I am pleased to meet you, Bolder," Jumper said.

Bolder moved out of the way to let Jumper into the room. Jumper looked all around the room, eventually meeting the gaze of his future allies. Jumper raised his arm and his hand slightly and waved gently.

"Hello! I am Jumper," Jumper said, his tone soothing and calm.

One of The Game Protectors chuckled, "We heard, Half-code."

One of Game Protectors stated mocking. This Game Protector was standing on the left. She was female, with long dark-red hair, a light gray skin tone, and black eyes. She wore a black undersuit, with a fairly reflective light blue armored chest piece. She also wore light blue armored gloves, which had a half-circle hole in them to put them on. Lastly, this Game Protector wore armored boots that were also light blue. These boots had wheels on both the inner and outer sides, and the wheels themselves had a silver and dark-blue checkered pattern on them.

Jumper tilted his hand to the right, and smiled, "What is your name?" Jumper asked the Game Protector who had mocked him.

"Racer. I master in swift-reflex combat," the Game Protector replied.

Jumper put out his hand, but she did not shake it.

"I hate the touch of Ethites," she said. Jumper clicked his tongue and turned around to meet the rest of The Game Protectors. He put his hands behind his back.

"You are an...Ethite," a Game Protector stated, filled with concern and confusion. He too wore the same armor and black undersuit that Racer had. His armor even had some of the same designs. However, his chest armor, boots, and gloves were light gray. Jumper tilted and nodded, "Respectfully, I would prefer if you all did not use that term, but...yes. I am a Glitch. At least...half a Glitch." Jumper regretfully agreed.

"I did not agree to have a Glitch on my squadron," the Game Protector shook his head. "You better prove yourself to me," the Game Protector snarled.

"You are the commander?" Jumper asked.

"That is correct," the Game Protector said.

"What is your name?" Jumper asked.

"Byte," Byte replied.

"The rumors were too good to be true! You...you are Tacitus's son!" Another Game Protector exclaimed somewhat calmly. His outfit was the same as the others, but the armor was yellow. "My name is Trip, the melee specialist."

Jumper nodded and smiled.

"Hi. I am Skyia, you Ethite," the air-specialist said.

"Silence! All of you! Let the poor man rest awhile. Let him rest before you lay judgment upon him," another Game Protector demanded. His voice was aged, and raspy. He was at the edge of the room, turned away from the others. He too wore the same armor and black undersuit that Racer had. It even had the same designs. However, his chest armor, boots, and gloves were bright orange. It was Eop.

"Eop of Ping-Pong?" Jumper asked.

"Yes. It is me. Say all the negative things you want. The Elder Game Protectors have already hurt me enough by demoting me and turning me into a ground soldier for Byte's Squadron. I have heard them all. All the insults. I care not anymore," Eop said.

"Oh sir! I would never!" Jumper stated, "I actually find favor with all that you have done. The inventive combat techniques, giving Glitches more and more freedoms! You are truly a revolutionary!" Jumper stopped, and sighed, "unfortunately no one gives you the credit," Jumper shook his head.

Eop smirked a little, "Thanks, what is your name again?" Eop inquired.

"Jumper."

Jumper Selects His Classes, December 1, 1999

Jumper sat on a bench just outside his dorm, and held a thin paper which listed the potential classes he could enroll in.

Jumper fidgeted with a blue pen in his hand; his eyes bulging at the paper, unsure of which classes to pick.

With one hand, Jumper drew his finger across the letters of the paper, mumbling what they said.

Off across the hall, Jumper began to hear loud trotting footsteps of a Game Protector walking by. Jumper looked up and saw that it was Bolder.

Bolder walked up to Jumper and asked if he could sit with him, and Jumper said yes. Bolder then sat down next to Jumper.

"What. Are. You. Doing?" Bolder asked, an emotionless rock.

"I am just-" Jumper sighed, "trying to figure out the last class I should enroll in."

"May. I. See. The. Sheet?" Bolder asked respectfully.

"Of course!" Jumper said, handing the sheet to Bolder.

"It is...Bolder, right?" Jumper asked.

Bolder nodded.

"How. About. Advanced. Defense?" Bolder asked. "You. Do. Not. Strike. Me. As. A. Violent. Type," Bolder stated.

"I will not until I fight you," Jumper smirked.

Bolder tilted his head.

"It is a joke!" Jumper laughed.

"Oh." Bolder realized, "I. Am. Not. Always. One. For. Emotions."

Jumper looked around the hallway, and then back at Bolder.

"Why are you so nice to me? I am an Ethite."

"Half. Of. One," Bolder smirked and chuckled.

"So, he does have a sense of humor," Jumper remarked.

"Sometimes." Bolder said, "I. Am. A. Fan. Of. The. Old. Ways. However. I. Do. Not. Believe. In. All. This. Persecution. And. Name. Calling. Of. Glitches. Honestly. I. Think. You. To. Be. A. Good. Person," Bolder admitted.

"Thank you, I needed that," Jumper said.

Bolder nodded, got up, and walked away. Jumper watched as he left, and then looked back at the paper. He then checked off Advanced Defense as his last class.

Jumper's First Class, December 3, 1999

"Good morning, class. Welcome to Advanced Defense," Eop boasted in a raspy, aged voice.

"Today is your first lesson, and you shall be paired up with each other to practice the moves I teach."

Eop proceeded to pair a couple of students up, making his way to Jumper. "Jumper," Eop called out, "You shall be paired with Racer."

Racer shook her head, "With'da Ethite? Ya' must be practicin' some comedy routine. I want no affiliation with tis' filth."

"Show some respect. He worked twice as hard as you just to get enrolled as a Game Protector," Eop defended.

Racer rolled her eyes and walked over to Jumper.

"What is ya' deal? Why become a Game Protector?" To fight ya' own kind?" Racer whispered to Jumper too fast for him to answer, but Eop spoke before he could answer.

"Let us begin class. I have chosen for Darrent and Forger, of the newer generation of Game Protectors, to demonstrate today's combat techniques. Watch with care," Eop commanded.

Darrent and Forger stood across from one another, their arms to their chests, and their hands open and loose.

"So, what ya' deal mate?"

"I have faced indifference my whole life. Game Protectors and Glitches would mock and say horrible things to me. Then...my father got arrested," Jumper admitted quietly.

"For bein' an Ethite?"

"No. Because he had relations with my mother Instilla, a Game Protector."

"So ya'r a Half-code-"

Jumper! Racer! Am I not currently teaching a lesson?" Eop scolded, "Do you think me unaware due to my age? That I did not hear you two discussing?"

"My apologies, sir," Jumper was quick to apologize.

"We're payin' attention! Well...'least I was. Dunno 'bout the Half-code over here."

"Is that right? Care to show me what I just taught?"

Racer walked over to Eop, and ushered Jumper to do the same.

"So...what'a we do?" Racer asked Eop.

"I thought I heard you say you were paying attention," Eop remarked with a smirk.

"Ha," Racer smiled and stood awkwardly.

Eop sighed, and shook his head, "Here, let me show you."

Eop lightly pressed Racer's palm back. "Put your fingers together, Eop tilted the angle of his head, "Bend your fingers slightly."

Racer did so.

"Good. Good." Eop remarked, "Now, Jumper, attempt to strike her."

"Strike me? His touch'll sicken me!" Racer screeched.

Eop looked at Racer as if she were a child. "Strike her, Jumper."

Jumper slowly flew his fist near Racer's palm; as Eop continued to guide Racer's palm. "Now, I am going to push your palm down just...slightly," Eop explained. "Your current grip will hypothetically block his attack for a short time. This gives you the opportunity to perform a counterattack."

Just as Eop taught, Jumper's fist was blocked by Racer's grip.

"Incredible!" Racer exclaimed.

"Not incredible yet," Eop chuckled. "Do the same move. Faster this time," Eop asked.

Both nodded.

Jumper and Racer looked at each other, intensely, pacing around one another in a circular fashion.

A Game Protector began tapping his foot on the ground, creating a chain reaction that turned into a beat. Into a chant.

Eop was about to raise his hand for silence, but he changed his mind; and smirked. He lowered his hand before the class could even see it.

Then the beat intensified and began to speed up. It was almost a non-verbal way of asking for either Jumper or Racer to strike. Jumper closed his eyes, breathed in, and then out.

Jumper heard a quick gust of wind fly near his face—an uncanny sound of a flying fist—and with eyes closed, he caught it. The tapping concluded, Jumper slowly opened his eyes, and he chuckled.

Racer's Discussion with Jumper, December 3, 1999

Jumper and Racer walked out of class together, and Racer—somewhat reluctantly—decided to share a dialogue with Jumper. She scoffed and sighed, finally saying: "I'll give you dis', Ethite. Ya'...do know how'ta put on a show."

Jumper laughed, "I actually was not trying to, but I suppose I did." Jumper paused a moment while they continued walking down the hallway. "To answer your previous questions, the reason I am doing this is—all of it—is because of my father, because of the mistreatment I; and many other Glitches, face. I want to put an end to it. Not get them arrested but achieve peace. I would like to see my father free again, and all those wrongfully imprisoned.

"I'm...surprised. I thought ya'r kind were barbaric an' emotionless. Monsters even. I mean ya'r only one of thousands, but'cha seem to have a just vision, even if it'a'be unrealistic right now."

The two shared a moment of silence.

"We'll see each other again. Nice talkin' wit'a," Racer admitted.

"I take it we are friends now?" Jumper asked.

Racer chuckled, "Not yet, but I'm warmin' up ta' ya'," she said as she walked away.

Jumper's Training in Watch Base 01, December 3-30, 1999

Jumper continued his training for many months, learning new combat strategies, and different offensive and defensive attacks.

"Try again, Jumper!" the Defensive Attacks teacher demanded of Jumper when he did an attack incorrectly. The attack in question was the "Darius Blockade."

This attack was first used by Darius "War" of Watch Base 01. Darius originally was a common thief, who—in order to survive and win on the streets—invented many unique combat techniques.

The first recorded use of the Darius Blockade was on February 13, 1976. Darius had just been seen stealing from the market, near a patrolling group of Game Protectors. He was cornered and had to think quickly.

Darius proceeded to put his left arm behind his back, secretly extending out his index and middle fingers. Almost at the same time, Darius covered his face with his right arm, preparing to be hit.

After taunting him for a good few moments, one of The Game Protectors attempted to strike Darius. Upon doing so however, The Game Protectors fist was waved away by Darius's right arm, and while the same Game Protector was stunned, Darius plunged his left arm—with his fingers still extended—into The Game Protectors mid-section.

Darius did not win that fight, however that was not entirely a loss for him. Seeing his ingenuity and ingeniousness, The Game Protectors decided to offer him a chance to join them rather than rotting away in a prison.

Though somewhat reluctant, Darius agreed to join the army, renaming himself "War" in the process.

For the next ten years, Darius continued to invent new combat techniques, before he went missing during an expedition to The Borderlands.

During a different class, another teacher shouted out: "Excellent Jumper!" This was the Aerial Attacks teacher, who complemented Jumper as he almost flawlessly performed the attack she had been teaching.

She had been teaching the class—and Jumper—the "Diving Dropdown" technique. This is an attack in which you jump up high, do a front-flip, and strike your enemy as you descend downward.

This attack was designed by Eop, though due to his "betrayal," he was not permitted to teach it nor take credit for its creation.

"Could be better, Ethite," the Ranged Attack teacher taunted and mocked Jumper, as he performed the "Enemy Calling" during his class.

This move is simply taunting your enemy from a distance, causing them to run right to you. If all goes to plan, you tighten your chest and stand still as the enemy races towards you. Once the enemy realizes that you are not moving; they will either try to stop themselves—resulting in tripping and falling to the ground, or being stunned and open for an attack as they try to balance—or crash right into you.

Jumper learned many other attacks such as the Double Additional Block, Singular Secular Block, and other attacks invented by Darius or Eop.

Jumper's Final Test and Formal Induction, December 31, 1999

A vast open field surrounded Jumper like a wide hug. Millions of beings crowded the seats, they were booing his name, their voices were echoing from every corner; he was surrounded, but alone.

The walls were a light tint of gray, bright in the eyes, and almost blinding Jumper, who had to cover his face with one of his arms. Tilting his head up to the infinite black sky, Jumper saw absolutely nothing. Pure soleness. This left Jumper with a feeling of solitude and sadness. It was a feeling akin to losing his father.

"Do you really believe yourself ready Jumper?" Byte snared, catching Jumper's attention, and bringing him back to reality.

Jumper looked at Byte and smirked, "I do not mean to sound cocky..." Jumper nodded his head, closed his eyes, and smiled, "I think I am ready," Jumper opened his eyes as he answered Byte.

Byte looked Jumper up and down. In Byte's eyes, he looked pathetic. Weak and thin gray armor like that of clothing; long thick black pants, and he was...barefoot? Surely, Byte could easily defeat him. He was nothing but an ignorant child.

Byte looked back at Jumper's face, yet again he was...smirking.

"What is so comical Jumper?" Byte snarled, ready to get this over with.

"Oh nothing! I am just," Jumper proceeded to burst into another smile, "excited to spar with you." Jumper stated in an odd manner. If was almost as if he was both cheerful...and calm.

Byte looked to the Elder Game Protectors, searching for approval.

Lead looked back and forth at his allies, they nodded slowly, and methodically. Lead grinned. He then extended his arm, his hand in a thumbed-up position. He nodded his head at Byte.

Like an arrow, Byte turned his head to Jumper and jolted right at him. Jumper stood chillingly still. Once Byte was no more than a meter away from Jumper, Jumper altered his stance. He put his left leg back, slightly squatted, tightened his chest, and pushed out his stomach.

Byte attempted to decelerate; however, it was no use. He ran head into Jumper. Byte stumbled backward, holding his head, but he was able to catch himself. Once he reevaluated his surroundings, he let go of his head. He looked at Jumper with immense agitation.

Abruptly and swiftly, Byte tried to punch Jumper, however Jumper closed his eyes, breathed in, and then out.

Jumper heard the quick gust of wind fly near his face—Byte's uncanny sound of Byte's flying fist—and with eyes closed, he caught it.

Jumper then let go, and Byte tripped, and fell head-first into the ground. The room erupted into disappointment, almost hatred.

After Byte laid on the ground a moment, Jumper grew concerned. He walked over to him slowly and carefully, and extended out his hand, "Byte...are you okay?" Jumper asked him, Byte painfully got into a kneeling position, "Yes." Byte paused and smirked behind Jumper's back, "I am fine!" Byte rapidly rotated around, and landed a clean strike on Jumper's jaw, propelling Jumper backward and onto the ground; the stadium boomed with cheer.

Jumper groaned as Byte stood himself up. Maliciously, he walked over to Jumper, each step perfectly planned and calculated. Byte laughed, "Not a smart move, Jumper." Byte said as he mocked Jumper with a shaking of the head.

Byte then bent over and prepared to strike Jumper a second time. As his fist came down like the swiftness of the sunset, a force blocked the blow. It was Jumper's left hand, which tightly grabbed Byte's punch similarly to a cage.

Jumper let go of Byte's fist, catching him off guard, and sending him tumbling back on the ground a second time.

Jumper was quick to spring back onto his feet, looking back at Byte, expecting victory. Instead, Byte reached out, and stabbed Jumper's legs with sharp, claw-like fingers. Byte pulled Jumper to the ground, right onto his head.

Once Jumper regained composure, he looked at Byte, who was staring back at him viciously.

"You are not the prophet, nor will you ever be," Byte barked at Jumper. He then proceeded to slam his head into Jumper's.

Byte stood up, his body aching.

"Though this man is clearly inexperienced, and undoubtedly unfit to call himself a Game Protector," Byte thought for a moment, "I shall yield." Byte nodded. "His training...is complete!" Byte exclaimed to the crowd.

Then Eop sat up from his viewing seat, his expression surprised, "A man shall yield to the prophet in battle."

The Elders and Byte's Squadron noticed this coincidence too, which began to spark confusion.

With his training fully complete, the ceremony commenced in which Jumper became an official Game Protector. During this Jumper got to choose a new armor set. This armor was like one that many other Game Protectors wore, except that it was red with a dark grey bodysuit underneath. That is the armor Jumper wore for the rest of his life.

Chapter 3 ...
THE START OF SOMETHING NEW

The Choosing of the Squadron for the Expedition to The Borderlands, January 3, 2000

Lead walked into the Meeting Room of Watch Base 01. The other Elder Game Protectors had been seated, waiting for Lead to arrive. Upon seeing him, they stood up, nodded their heads, and with respect said; "Commander."

Lead nodded his head modestly in reply.

"You all may be seated," Lead stated.

The Elder Game Protectors proceeded to sit back down.

"I assume we are going to discuss this year's squadron candidate for the Expedition to The Borderlands." Vice said.

"Precisely," Lead agreed.

"Is it not time that we finally relieve ourselves of the duty? To quit sending soldiers to a pointless, and impossible, mission?" Protect argued.

Lead tilted his head for a moment, pulled his chair out, and sat down. He thought and looked at Protect: "Perhaps it is time to finally let go. Even still, we should at least try one last time. I have a feeling that...this time will be different.

"Then which squadron shall we choose?" Dawn asked.

Lead tilted his head again and lifted it down. He then tapped his fingers on the table ahead of him. He looked up at the room: "Byte's Squadron."

The room erupted into both shock and anger.

"Byte's Squadron!" Upside exclaimed.

"They are some of the best soldiers that we have!" Dawn fought.

"Exactly!" Lead brought the room back to silence. "All this time we have been wasting their talents! Perhaps they could be the squadron who finally completes this task!" Lead defended.

"What of their new member? What was it...Jumper?" Protect asked.

"Jumper!" Vice growled, "that kid is a rookie! Incapable of defeating our most skilled soldier, let alone an army of Glitches! Worst of all, he is a Dadum Ethite!"

"Perhaps that is not such a bad thing! An Ethite interacting with other Ethites? That is exactly what we need! Someone from our ranks who can relate to their ranks. Perhaps a deal could be made because of Jumper," Lead again defended.

"Or he could betray us," Vice stammered.

"He could... but he has no reason to do so. At least, none that I can think of. He seems...loyal."

The room grew silent once again, and then Lead asked: "So, are we in agreement?" Lead asked.

The Elder's nodded.

"Good. I will send a messenger to Byte's Squadron. They will depart in a few days."

The Call for the Expedition to The Borderlands, January 3, 2000

Byte's Squadron had been in their quarters, each member having a separate conversation with another. Jumper was talking with Bolder about his training and induction, Trip was discussing with Eop of the olden days and times, and Skyia and Racer were playfully arguing about whether aerial or ground combat was better.

As for Byte, he was sitting at his desk working and participated in none of the ongoing conversations.

Jumper noticed Byte was alone and interrupted his conversation with Bolder to check on Byte: "Commander Byte, I do not mean to offend you, but...you look lonely. Would you like to join Bolder and my conversation?"

Byte bit his lower lip and shook his head: "No I would not. But...thank you, Jumper."

The door began vibrating as one knocked on it. Bolder turned his head to look at the door, walked over, and opened it.

"Good evening," a Game Protector Messenger said. His face had stubble, and he was...fairly young. His eyes were somewhat dull with a piercing bright orange squint, his hair was black like a midnight sky, and he was wearing a one-piece, blue suit, with a circular badge. The badge had a silver rim, and a red center.

"May I speak with your commander?"

Though Bolder thought the man was a little young to be a messenger, he chose to keep his thoughts in; and said nothing. Bolder nodded to the man's request of coming inside the room, and stepped aside to let the man come in.

The man proceeded to walk up to Byte who stood up and shook the messenger's hand.

"Good evening, Commander Byte. I have a message from the Elder Game Protectors."

"Do tell."

The messenger leaned over and whispered the message into Byte's ear. Byte almost immediately collapsed back into his chair in shock.

"Commander Byte, are you okay?" the messenger asked.

"Yes. Thank you," Byte waved his hand to signal the messenger to leave. The messenger did so.

Once the door was closed, Racer looked at Byte with concern: "What'e he say?"

The room stayed quiet for a moment.

"We have been chosen for the expedition to The Borderlands."

The Departure from Watch Base 01, January 6, 2000

Trumpets blew in the wind as Byte's Squadron moved toward the exit of the city. Blocked by fences, townsfolk cheered on the guards and shouted at the squadron.

Even still, insults and comments polluted the air, specifically towards Jumper.

"This Ethite does not deserve to be a Game Protector!" a citizen shouted in angst.

"Hopefully this Half-code parishes in The Borderlands!" another citizen exclaimed.

Paired with these insulting words, were signs which too ridiculed and mocked Jumper.

On the other hand, those who supported Byte, Bolder, or the other members of the squadron, praised them.

"Bolder is the greatest warrior I have ever seen!"

"Byte is fit beyond all reason to be a commander!"

"Did you hear? Racer can dispatch and dispose thousands of Ethites in mere seconds!"

They too, had signs to match, but these signs were ones of positivity, and respect.

Jumper then saw a man with red-tinted-eyes; a sign of one being a demon or possessed. It is for this reason that the crowd sprinted past him, that jobs were denied to him, and that his family excommunicated him at birth. He now laid against a building, begging for coins.

"Stop," Jumper raised his arm, his hand open, "We shall help him."

"Half-code!" Racer shouted in a whisper, "He is a Lectin!"

Jumper turned to face his squadron members: "Most of you are quick to judge. Only a select few of you have true patience. Patience to look past one's oddities and appreciate their skills rather than their race." Jumper looked around at his squadron members and prepared to increase his volume so that everyone around him could hear: "I say to you that anyone who treats another poorly for an unwarranted reason is the corrupt one," Jumper exclaimed, as he spun around, looking at the citizens of Watch Base 01. Jumper then pointed at the man with his red-tinted eyes: "This man is no demon, nor a possessed one. If you think otherwise just look to me and notice my garments. I too have the color red displayed on me, yet nobody sees it as harmful," Jumper paused. "This man, just like the rest of you, is a Game Protector; and should not be treated as anything other than that."

Jumper walked over to the man: "and if my words do not ring true to you, I shall prove it to you."

Jumper crouched down to the man's level, and whispered: "May I?"

The man stared deeply into Jumper's eyes and realized he was to do no harm to him, and so the man nodded in agreement.

"Close your eyes." Jumper instructed kindly, and the man did so.

Jumper proceeded to gently place his thumbs on the man's eyelids, and press. After a moment, Jumper removed his thumbs, and the man opened his eyes. Those watching, and Byte's Squadron all gasped in amazement, as the man's eyes were now a bright blue color. Byte was taken back by all the attention Jumper was receiving because of his miracle and began to grow jealous of him as a result.

The man placed his fingers on his cheek, and then he turned to see his reflection in a window. Softly, he whispered: Thank you," as he continued to be enamored by what Jumper had done to him.

Jumper smiled, nodded his head, and stood up. Jumper turned back to face the rest of Byte's Squadron, but in doing so, he caught a glimpse of the Elder Game Protector Lead, who had seen the entire miracle performed. Jumper's smile quickly faded. Jumper then walked back into the squadron.

"The prophet shall heal a Lectin," Eop murmured.

Byte's Squadron then made it to the tall, and reflective, silver gate. It was as if the gate was intentionally designed to intimidate enemies, as it had cylinder rods with spikes upon the tops of almost every cylinder. It almost looked like that of a jail cell.

Two guards proceeded to a different side of the gate. One going left and one going right, in order to open both doors.

Tightly gripping the handle of the gate door, they used all their might to open the mighty heavy door. Now with both gates open, they signaled Byte's Squadron to come forward and leave Watch Base 01.

The Arrival to The Borderlands of Superworld, February 15, 2000

The Game Protectors saw The Borderlands at a distance. The poor, discolored, gloomy, and depressing part of The Superworld. A place in which The Developers left almost entirely unattended, but still cared for. In the distance was a dark gray mountain, a mountain in which Lee-Der found residence. Around the mountain were houses. Compared to the rich and wonderful houses of The Game Protectors, these houses held no bounds. These houses were cheaply made, poorly designed, and crafted using the unused assets in which The Developer's discarded.

Byte's Squadron had an uneasy feeling approaching this area of the world. They felt as if they would be attacked at any moment. The only member of Byte's Squadron that didn't feel this way was Jumper.

"This place is quite... disgusting," Byte snarled, his voice filled with hate. Jumper looked at Byte with an offended facial expression: "Who are you to say that?" Jumper asked, his tone making his rightful anger on inequality shown. Byte and his squadron stopped, and Byte closed his eyes and breathed in. Byte turned around slowly and menacingly. He faced Jumper. It was clear he was filled with fury. "Respectfully Byte, as much as you despise The Glitches, and how much you despise me, you have to see the truth: The Glitches are beings too. Beings The Developers let into this world." Jumper said confidently, standing his ground against Byte, and showing a serious face. "They are criminals Jumper!" Byte exclaimed, no longer holding in his anger. "They are only criminals because that is the only option The Game Protectors ever gave them." Jumper said, remaining calm and content. Byte ignored Jumper and turned to face the Glitch's houses.

Jumper's Speech at The Borderlands, February 15, 2000

Glitches slowly began to walk out of their homes. They carried spears, pitchforks, swords. They hid their curious children behind them, making a wall to ensure their safety. They were prepared. Prepared for The Game Protectors to attack. Then, Lee-Der emerged out of the darkness. Each footstep Lee-Der made echoed loudly throughout his cave.

Then, a symphony of booming drums played, and with every beat of the drum, another one of Lee-Der's steps followed. The Game Protectors quickly turned their heads towards the band, almost giving themselves whiplash. The band in question was using even more unused assets for their instruments. The drums themselves were made out of trash cans, and tree branches served as their sticks in which The Glitches played the drums.

All of this commotion came to a screaming halt as soon as Lee-Der finally revealed himself. Lee-Der raised both of his hands in the air, with his palms open, in facing the Game Protectors. Lee-Der then commanded the band to stop by swiftly lowering his hands and closing his eyes. There was a minute of utter silence.

Lee-Der then opened his eyes: "I had promised this day long ago. The day in which a treaty of peace would finally present itself." Lee-Der boasted, confident in his words, "That day comes with him!" Lee-Der exclaimed, pointing at Jumper.

Jumper in turn, tried to get in front of Byte, but Byte turned around, and stopped him: "Jumper!" Byte said in a loud whisper, "Do not quarrel with this Ethite. Do not disregard or argue with me again, or I will have you face dangerously large consequences," Byte threatened in a menacing way.

"You." Lee-Der said, his voice agitated, as he pointed at Byte, "I demand to talk with this man, if you prohibit me to do so, I may just let Settings, my first lieutenant, rework your programming," Lee-Der too threatened.

Byte thought, *"But I am the leader of this squadron. Why would you not want to talk to me?"* Byte grew even more jealous of Jumper. Byte then, reluctantly, moved out of the way. Jumper walked one step up. "I do not know you, but I do know this: "You are no Game Protector, nor a Glitch. What are you then?" Lee-Der questioned.

"I am...a little-bit of both," Jumper chuckled.

Lee-Der too laughed, and The Glitches gasped loudly, some even called Jumper names. "Fonte!" a Glitch screamed in anger, "Half-code!" a group of Glitches exclaimed in unison.

"Silence!" Lee-Der ordered to The Glitches, "Did I not say that this man will bring us peace?" Lee-Der shouted to The Glitches. "Are you speaking the truth? That you are a Half-code?" Lee-Der questioned.

"Yes, sir, I am," Jumper responded. "My mother Instilla, and my father Tacitus, were in fact married right around here," Jumper explained.

"Yes!" Lee-Der remembered, "They were."

Lee-Der then tilted his head and thought for a moment. "I am sure it is not easy, you must...face a lot of...racism?" Lee-Der said, trying to understand Jumper's situation. "I suppose then, I shall listen to you. I do speculate you have an offer of peace, do you not?" Lee-Der asked Jumper.

"I do. You come with us to Watch Base 01, not to be arrested but to be given citizenship; to have freedom. Of course, those who truly did commit crimes would face sentencing, but those who did not...I promise to fight for you, defend you."

"A fair deal," Lee-Der admitted, "But...can we truly trust you?"

"I cannot prove my words, so I shall demonstrate my trust in another fashion."

Jumper breathed in and closed his eyes. Then, a few seconds later, all of the weapons all of the Game Protector's carried flew into The Glitches' hands: leaving every member on the squadron unarmed.

Jumper opened his eyes.

"The prophet shall disarm an army," Eop whispered to himself.

"We all are now defenseless, with your army fully armed. In what other way could we show our combined trust?" Jumper said rhetorically.

Lee-Der smirked and nodded. "Is every Glitch in favor of the Half-code's plan?"

Though some disagreed, most Glitches were in awe of Jumper, and in a consensus with Jumper.

"It is decided. We come with you," Lee-Der stated.

Byte's Squadron gasped and shook their heads in disbelief. They were now closer to believing Jumper was the prophet.

Eop mumbled under his breath, words from his memory: "...the Prophet will unite Glitches and Game Protectors alike; in paradise."

Chapter 4...
THE BEGINNING OF THE END

The Return to Watch Base 01, March 18, 2000

Horns blew, and townsfolk cheered as the menacing spike-topped gates squealed open. Marching proud and upright, Byte's Squadron along with The Glitches, returned, waving and greeting the excited citizens.

Ahead of them, in the center of the city, was a stage. On it, were the Elder Game Protectors, nodding with their hands behind their backs.

Finally reaching the center of the city, The Game Protectors stopped and waited for the Elders to speak.

"Today is a glorious day!" Lead boasted, "A day that shall be recorded for the next many decades." Lead paused, "This squadron has not only accomplished a feat that no one has yet achieved, but they also did it without any fatalities. Excellent work. Truly, excellent."

Byte signed, reluctance filled his breath, "I would like to say it is true commander, that we did this as a squadron, but it is simply not true. Jumper...he convinced The Glitches to come with us. He did so all in one speech; one he performed on his own."

The crowd gasped, "Jumper, come forward," Lead commanded.

Jumper came closer to the stage, "Is this true?" Lead asked.

"Though I refrain from boasting of it, it is," Jumper admitted. "I made a deal with The Glitches, that you only arrest those of them who truly committed a crime. That does not include their flee from prison. You are also to give them proper citizenship here in Watch Base 01," Jumper explained.

The Elders looked at each other and nodded.

"Though we do not appreciate you demanding orders from us...given that you finished this over-lingering mission, we will accept you and The Glitches' request. The Glitches shall be given refuge here in Watch Base 01."

Glitches and Game Protector's alike, cheered Jumper on, most proclaiming him to be the prophet, or, at the very least, giving him many loud compliments.

"Just as the prophecy stated!" a citizen shouted.

"Jumper is the prophet!" another proclaimed.

"What an accomplished young man!" an elderly citizen said.

"Truly, Jumper must be the prophet," Eop mumbled. Then, without Eop even realizing, members of Byte's Squadron nodded in agreement with him. However...Byte, did not.

Jumper Foretells the Fulfillment of the Prophecy, March 18, 2000

Byte's Squadron returned to their dorm, faith filling the air.

Bolder closed the dorm door once everyone was in, and they all circled Jumper; except for Byte, whom was once again at his desk: working.

Jumper smiled, "What are you all doing?"

"It's pretty clear Jumper. All the signs, all the miracles, gettin' The Glitches ta' come here, unite wit' us," Racer begun, "Ya' half ta' be the prophet."

"She is right. There are too many coincidences, too many elements to ignore. Jumper...we all believe you are the prophet," Eop stated.

"And. We. Are. Here. To. Help. You. Listen. To. You. Do. Whatever. You. Ask. If. You. Will. Have. Us," Bolder explained.

"Well, not all of us," Byte said.

"Byte, be respectful. Jumper is obviously the prophet," Racer said.

"While I don't argue with you, Racer, Jumper has also disregarded me and seemingly tried to take my place as leader of this Squadron," Byte responded, his eyes bulging and his heart full of anger.

"What's wrong with that? No offense, Byte, but Jumper has shown more qualities of being a leader then I believe you have." Eop added in.

Then Byte looked at him angrily without saying a word and stormed out.

Jumper smiled, and did not say anything for a moment. He then looked over to Racer.

"Are we friends yet?" Jumper smiled.

"I'm gonna follow ya', not be friends, " Racer chuckled.

Jumper smirked and shook his head. He then walked into the middle of the circle.

Jumper clasped his hands together around his stomach, bowed his head to his new followers, and closed his eyes. Upon lifting his head back up, and gently opening his eyelids, he spoke:

"A war is coming," Jumper opened chillingly, "a war in which most who come to believe in me...will not survive." Jumper, paused, letting his words sink in. The Game Protectors looked at each other with confusion and a tad bit of fear.

Jumper noticed this, and was motivated to reassure that everything will work out for the best: "But worry, not! For this is how the prophecy must be fulfilled!" Jumper explained and reassured.

"For the Elder Game Protectors, and The Glitches, will unite over a war against their common enemy. A common enemy in which is...me," Jumper continued, and then paused again, emotion overflowed in his face: "It is in this way...that the....prophecy will be fulfilled." Jumper struggled to say. "So, I say to you now: continue to follow me, my teachings, and take note of my miracles. Enjoy it now. For the path that I follow, and the one you all have chosen will not be easy. But give up not, and even when you lose sight of me, have faith that I am with you; for trust me I am. I am with you, always."

Jumper then walked out of the circle and went on to the balcony. He closed the door behind him, and he wept.

Jumper Prophesizes his Death, Watch Base 01, Match 18, 2000

Bolder saw Jumper walk out, and after a few moments of looking at the Followers of Jumper, and the balcony door, he decided to go after Jumper. He proceeded to the balcony door, and slid it open, closing it behind him.

Jumper stared off into the distance, looking at the city of The Game Protectors, looking at Watch Base 01.

Jumper heard Bolder coming and tilted his head to think. Jumper then said what was on his mind: "From this view, you truly begin to see how little the problems we face are," Bolder, who had been walking up to Jumper slowly, stopped in his tracks. "Those. Are." Bolder paused, and dropped the old way of speaking, "Great words Jumper, but something is troubling me right now." Bolder reluctantly let himself chuckle at his statement.

"It really must be, if you are talking this way. What is troubling you?" Jumper replied turning around, to face his friend. His arms still behind him, holding on to the balcony's railway, and leaning on it.

"You know more then you are telling us," Bolder turned his head, "am I wrong?" Bolder said with a stern facial expression, and a serious voice. Jumper chuckled and smiled. Jumper then turned around and thought for a moment. Jumper turned his head back to Bolder, "I am afraid that you are not," Jumper said, his tone shifting into depression.

"I die, Bolder. That is how the prophecy is fulfilled; with my death."

Bolder's face reflected a shocked and worried expression, but he said nothing.

"There is one other thing," Jumper began. "You are going to force your beliefs onto someone, the man who will help me fulfill the prophecy." Jumper admitted reluctantly, his words struggling to remove themselves from Jumper's lips.

"I am not one to show emotion, let alone anger or force," Bolder paused, tilting his head in curiosity: "How does this happen?" Bolder asked, confused.

Jumper responded: "On that day, you will see me laying on the ground. You will see him, see the man who is to kill me, and you will attack him without forethought. With a voice lashing out, you will cry out words of force. You will not give the man any choice but to believe in me, and if he does not do so, you will prepare to kill him. You will make yourself no different from those who will be persecuting you." Jumper stated coldly.

Bolder stood for a moment, thinking. He breathed heavily, and then started to walk back into the room to collect his thoughts. "Hey, Bolder," Jumper said.

"Yes?"

"You do not have to hide your emotions. No longer should you. Use your emotions to drive you; not into horrible deeds, but ones of good," Jumper said. "This may seem contradictory though, as I do not want you to use anger as a motive. Embrace your emotions but stay away from anger," Jumper taught.

Bolder nodded, "You are right Jumper. Thank you, I...I do not want to see you perish. You are my friend, my greatest friend." "It is the way it has to be," Jumper said.

Bolder still held in some sorrow, but managed to say: "Goodnight, Jumper."

"Goodnight, my friend," Jumper replied, and Bolder went back inside.

The Growth in Faith, March 18-December 2, 2000

For the next months, more and more heard of everything Jumper had done; from his miracles, few teachings, and managing to call upon The Glitches to return to Watch Base 01.

Jumper was being written into history accounts. evangelized by townsfolk on the streets as the prophet. The more recognized he was, the more most of the Elder Game Protectors distanced themselves from him. They began to send out messengers to attempt to disprove Jumper's teachings and his position as the prophet. Jumper easily refuted these messengers on a mission to discredit him and spoke out against many of the Elder Game Protectors for their cowardly ways of speaking through others. Little by little, more and more came to believing Jumper to be the prophet, and though many still despised Jumper, he was quickly gaining popularity.

Jumper continued to walk amongst the streets, teaching, preaching, and foreshadowing the events to come.

As for Byte, he only grew more hatred for Jumper, as his squadron began treating him less as a leader, and more of an average solider. Not only that, but he did not believe Jumper to be the prophet, and thought all those claiming him to be; were speaking heresy.

Lee-Der and Byte's Betrayal

December 2, 2000

Lee-Der looked up to see Byte rage—fully standing in the hallway leading to his office. "You may come in," Lee-Der stated calmly to Byte. Byte walked in quickly, making each footstep known. He then proceeded to slam both of his open palms on Lee-Der's desk: "Why call me in here? Why not Jumper. You seem to be all ears to his opinions," Byte said, his voice loud, furious, and agitated. Lee-Der laughed at him.

"You think I care for Jumper? Sure, the young man is obviously wise beyond anything I have seen, but that is not exactly why

163

you were called here." Lee-Der continued, sounding as if he was about to start negotiating with Byte. Byte was aware of this.

"Enough with your pathetic and sorrowful tactics, Ethite!" Byte raised his voice, his patience wearing thin.

"Careful with offenses...I might not make my deal with you," Lee-Der breathed in, struggling to maintain a calming attitude.

"What deal?" Byte's body bounced backward, his head tilted vertically, he was confused. His tone changed to that of a questioning one. "When I took a glance at Jumper for the first time, I listened to his words; and well...they were revolutionary. The Elder Game Protectors, and even some of the younger ones, are not a fan of that—yourself included," Lee-Der began.

"You sound as if...you're going to exploit that," Byte smirked, and chuckled.

"I personally do not believe Jumper is the Prophet, nor do I believe in the prophecy. Therefore, I think he speaks blasphemy, I am tired of hearing of his so-called miracles and so are the Elder Game Protectors. They talked to me, and said if I deal with Jumper, me and my Glitches will revive more freedom in Watch Base 01," Led-Der explained.

"Did Jumper not do that for you?" Byte asked frustrated.

"We are still not permitted into the military and are severely mistreated in all other senses. I know Jumper said he would take care of this for us, but I know even he does not have that much influence; especially now that the Elders are beginning to hate him and his followers," Lee-Der paused.

"I will help you, Lee-Der. Only because Jumper has taken everything from me," Byte stated.

Chapter 5...
IN THE END

The Attempted Burning of the Followers of Jumper, December 3, 2001

Smoke filled the dorm room, and Bolder coughed, causing him to awaken. He sat up from his rest and noticed a blazing fire emerging from a distance.

"Wake up! Everybody wake up! There is a fire!"

One by one everyone in the Byte's Squadron woke up, and upon seeing the situation; attempted to escape. However, some kind of log appeared to have fallen and blocked the front entrance, leaving them trapped.

Bolder looked over his shoulder, and realized Jumper, continued in slumber, almost completely unaware of the fire.

"Jumper!" Bolder screamed.

"Yes, Bolder?" Jumper asked in a faint and half-awake voice.

"Do you not see! There is a fire ahead of us. It will surely end us all if we do nothing to stop it!" Bolder yelled in an almost anxious voice.

"You all are quick to worry. It is clear proof you do not trust in my abilities," Jumper said.

"We are in a dire situation. Please, Jumper, help!" Trip yelled.

Jumper sat up, and waited for a moment.

"What'ya doin? Help!" Racer screamed.

"Please, be patient. Have faith," Jumper remarked.

He then lifted his hand and angled it, closing his eyes. Suddenly, a boisterous roaring wind came from the sky, and into the fire. It was immediately put out.

"The prophet shall calm a fire..." Eop mumbled under his breath.

"Open the door now, it has been cleared from the log," Jumper asked.

Bolder opened the door with ease; as if no log had blocked it.

Jumper rose to his feet, and guided his comrades through the hallways, to the exit. They were all in shock and awe.

They managed to get outside.

"Ya' saved all of us Jumper, ya' saved me! I'm sorry for my doubt," Racer remarked.

"Me. As. Well." Bolder calmed back down.

"It is okay, you both did not know," Jumper reassured.

"What of Byte? Where is he?" Trip asked the team.

Jumper pointed to a building not too far from their dorm. Upon this silver cylinder of a building was a balcony, and you could clearly see both Lee-Der and Byte standing atop of the balcony, staring down at the Followers of Jumper. "He is there. He made a deal to betray us. To betray...me," Jumper revealed.

The Escape of the Followers of Jumper, December 3, 2001

With Jumper ahead, leading the exodus, his followers followed him. The group stayed silent, not sharing a singular word amongst each other. This made the sound of their footsteps crystal clear, echoing around the landscape. After seven-and-a-quarter miles, the group finally had enough time to reflect on the previous events; and busted into a clan of furry-filled activists. "I cannot believe that Nero Byte betrayed us!" Trip exclaimed, full of anger and resentment, and the side conversations, and muddled chatter began.

"He was no good leader!" Skyia yelled furiously.

"He must die for what he has done!" Racer angrily stated, with the crowd agreeing with her in a loud cheer. Jumper stopped. For a moment, the chattering continued, booming throughout The Superworld, but once every person had realized Jumper stopped, so did their lips. Once Jumper heard no more words in the air, he breathed in, closed his eyes, and turned around.

"Is it not written that you mustn't seek revenge? Or that anger is not permitted?" Jumper asked the crowd rhetorically. They did not answer. "Is it not also written that you must treat others with respect, including your enemies?" Jumper continued.

"What would'ya have us do then?" Racer asked swiftly.

"I ask that you worry not of the future, or the past. Do not seek revenge or go on a hero's journey. Rather, continue to follow me. Continue my mission of peace. Do not let the beginnings of persecution dwindle your faith or lead you astray. My mission is nearly complete. The Game Protectors and Glitches are almost living in harmony together."

Jumper paused, allowing his words to sink in.

"Why do I think this mission is nearly complete if not already finished? Well...I believe myself to be the prophet. I also believe that I have shown there is proof to my claims; through the miracles I have performed," Jumper paused again.

And for those who are yet to see my miracles," Jumper smiled, "keep watching."

The Start of the Persecution, December 3, 2001

Words of the arson spread widely throughout the town, and protesting began.

The protesting, however, was not in defense of the Followers of Jumper. Rather, in offense of the Followers of Jumper. It almost seemed as if the fire was the final push needed, to have almost every citizen turn on Jumper and his Followers, not that most were not already turned against them from the start.

Signs cursed Jumper and his Followers, saying how they should have; and deserved to have, perished in the fire. Signs that cursed Jumper, calling him an Ethite, and a false prophet.

Then, it got worse. Those who even spoke one positive word of Jumper were cornered. They would then either be killed or assaulted by a group of non-believers. A group which sometimes were made of Glitches and Game Protectors; something never seen before.

The Followers of Jumper constantly had to keep tight the guard, as even if they stepped one foot outside, something horrible would occur, whether it be something non-harmful as mockery, or something as brutal as a full-fledged attempted assault.

As for the Elder Game Protectors, they did not seem to care about all of the persecution. If anything, they almost promoted it, even if they did so indirectly.

Although they never do it directly, the Elders never stopped sending out Messengers to speak out against Jumper, in order to not directly be affiliated with the Followers of Jumper; or Jumper himself.

In response, Jumper continued to directly combat the Elders, and their timid and non-confrontational methods. Jumper also spoke out how the Elder's disrespected and twisted the prophecy into their own liking. How the prophecy never said Glitches would be eradicated, but rather live in peace alongside The Game Protectors.

Jumper continued to do these actions, as well as perform miracles, until the war started.

By this time, the persecution was intense, and it was clear revolution would begin. Though reluctant, The Glitches and The Game Protectors began to ally more frequently; arguing and protesting to the Elders that Jumper—and his followers—were both an enemy of Watch Base 01, and an enemy of The Developers.

The protesters continued to push the Elders to arrest Jumper, and after not much convincing, the Elders officially declared Jumper, and his Followers, enemies of Watch Base 01 and The Developers. Their declaration: Jumper was to be arrested, killed, or exiled, and so too were his followers.

Jumper's Decision, December 3, 2001

Jumper and his followers took refuge in a small apartment. "It is time," Jumper stated chillingly. "All of you split up! Run! Do whatever you can to avoid the wrath. You may all believe, and trust in me; but this is not your battle to conquer. It is mine. Leave it to me."

"Jumper...what are you talking about?" Trip asked.

"I told you not long ago, that in the coming days, the prophecy will be fulfilled. Today is that day. My body and soul will perish in the fight that I cannot win, and the moment I die...unity will be achieved."

"You'a gonna die?" Racer was shocked with fear and disbelief. "No. No. No!" She shook her head.

"Jumper...we cannot let you go!" Bolder argued, his voice almost cracked, "surely there is another way."

"Bolder..." Jumper reassured, "I have prayed, and asked The Developers if there is any other way. This is my destiny." Jumper shed a tear.

"Goodbye...Jumper," Trip bowed his head and shook Jumper's hand.

"Farewell, Prophet," Eop said, bowing his head in respect.

Jumper stuck out his hand, and Eop shook his hand.

"I...take we are friends now?" Racer slowed her voice and stuck out her arm for Jumper to shake.

Jumper smirked, "Of course," he said as he shook her hand.

"I bid you well," Skyia nodded her head. She was still in shock.

"I really...must be going," Jumper admitted, his voice reluctant.

182

Bolder held back his emotions, but you could see sadness seep through his helmet and language, "Good...goodbye, Jumper," Bolder said, shaking his hand.

Jumper then walked over to the door, opened it, looked back for a moment, and he left; knowing what he had to do.

Jumper Versus Lee-Der, December 3, 2001

"The so-called prophet," Lee-Der said, smiling, and chuckling. Jumper stared at him with a blank expression, thinking about what it was he was going to say. Jumper breathed in, and then out, and answered: "I forgive you Lee-Der, I forgive you and your allies for persecuting my followers," Jumper stopped. "However, I won't allow your deeds to go unpunished. If I must defend my disciples, then I will defend them."

"If you truly believe yourself to be the Prophet Jumper, you cannot stop me. For it is written, "The prophet will never strike first...wait," Lee-Der begun to state, but realized he had misinterpreted the readings.

Jumper's expression changed to that of a smile. "The prophet is, in fact, allowed to defend his followers if he so chooses," Jumper smiled. Not in an arrogant or malicious way, but in a kind, and reassuring way. He smiled in order to inform Lee-Der his thoughts of misinterpreting the readings were right.

However, Jumper's smile slowly disappeared, and his eyes rolled down as he thought of his next statement. Jumper took a few moments to pause, and then said: "I do not want to hurt you Lee-Der."

Jumper's eyes rolled back up, and faced Lee-Der, "but I will do what is necessary to protect the beliefs of my followers. The right of religion is a right in which everyone should have. What you have faith in shouldn't be forced onto others if they choose not to accept it, no matter how right you may think you are." Jumper explained, trying to persuade Lee-Der, even though he knew it may not work.

"What of you then Jumper? Why are you free to defend your beliefs and I am not?" Lee-Der inquired. "There is a difference between your actions and mine, Lee-Der. Your followers have attacked mine. You have resolved to violence, whereas I have barely laid a finger on your followers. The only instance in which I would attack your Glitches was to defend myself, and my disciples," Jumper answered.

Lee-Der lowered his head, and took a moment to think about what Jumper was saying. "I suppose that's true..." Lee-Der raised his head, and his gaze meets Jumper's gaze, "but...you...cannot be the...prophet." Lee-Der said with uncertainty, whilst shaking his head slowly, beginning to question his actions.

"I...I..refuse to believe it!" Lee-Der stated with a shaken voice, not fully believing in what he was saying.

"That is your choice, and if you must cut me down, feel free to do so," Jumper stated in a calm, and near-silent voice. Lee-Der separated his feet apart, fixed his posture, and raised his feet to his hands. His hands were now in a clinched position. Lee-Der almost started running, but stopped as he heard Jumper slightly shout "But!"

Jumper allowed Lee-Der to take a moment to Re-situate himself. "Know if you strike me and my followers down," Jumper paused, "You are no better than The Game Protectors who persecuted you," Jumper finished.

Lee-Der took a moment to ponder, to think if this is really the best course of action. He then put one foot in front of the other in quick succession, going for speed. He attacked Jumper.

The Final Fight at Watch Base 01, December 3, 2001

After taunting him for a good few moments, Lee-Der attempted to strike Jumper. Upon doing so however, Jumper crossed his arms near his chest, in the shape of the letter X. Jumper then extended his right index finger and arched it slightly. Next, he extended out his thumb, keeping it straight, followed by swinging out his right arm, keeping his thumb and index finger in the same position, catching Lee-Der's first strike. However, Lee-Der tried hitting Jumper again, so Jumper swung out his left arm, and hit Lee-Der. Lee-Der was knocked back, and then stood back his ground.

As Lee-Der came toward Jumper, Jumper stood still. Jumper proceeded to put his left arm behind his back, secretly extending out his index and middle fingers. Almost at the same time, Jumper covered his face with his right arm, preparing to be hit.

Lee-Der's fist was waved away by Jumper's right arm, and while Lee-Der was stunned, Jumper plunged his left arm—with his fingers still extended—into Lee-Der's mid-section.

Lee-Der was stunned, giving Jumper some time to put distance between him and his target.

As Lee-Der jolted toward Jumper, Lee-Der was about arms-length away from Jumper, he jolted. Jumper watched his opponent. Lee-Der reached his right arm out, turning his hand into a fist. Swiftly, Jumper retracted his arms, his palms revealed, and his fingers slightly bent. Jumper slid to the right side, tilting his head to the right as well. Lee-Der landed in a kneeling position, his fist crashing into the ground, and his head vertically turning to meet Jumper. Lee-Der then attempted to backhand Jumper using his left arm, however Jumper quickly reacted. Jumper crossed his arms into an X and moved his head to the left to embrace for impact.

Once Lee-Der's arm made contact with Jumper's crossed arms, Jumper violently slid backwards. Lee-Der then quickly raised his right arm, his fist still clenched and twisted his back. Lee-Der proceeded to once again hit Jumper vigorously.

Jumper spun around due to the attack and stumbled slightly. Lee-Der took this quick opportunity to stand, and while Jumper struggled to find balance, Lee-Der walked up to Jumper and wound up his right arm to strike him again.

Jumper regained his balance and heard Lee-Der growl as he attempted to hit him. Jumper swiftly turned around, and crouched down, watching Lee-Der perform his attack. Lee-Der too was staring at Jumper, with a frustrated expression. Lee-Der then tried to punch downward with his left arm, but Jumper rolled out of the way. Jumper ended up on his back, his arms close to his face, and his fingers bent.

Jumper saw Lee-Der ahead of him, and believed he had enough time to get up. Jumper quickly rolled to his side, planted his right hand on the ground, and lifted himself into a kneeling position.

Jumper was then struck violently in the head by Lee-Der's left hand. Jumper fell to the right, onto his back.

Lee-Der attempted to hit Jumper in the head again, but Jumper raised his hands to his face to block it. Jumper then quickly proceeded to roll over to the right again.

This time, Jumper sprang up into a standing position, carefully eyeing his surroundings. He ensured Lee-Der did not sneak up on him again.

Lee-Der then flew a fist toward Jumper's head. Jumper simply avoided the fist, then grabbed Lee-Der's arm—with all his might—and used his head to stun Lee-Der, by hitting his face.

Lee-Der agitatedly stared at Jumper, as he tried to regain composure. Jumper looked back at him calculatingly.

"Is this really what you want Lee-Der?" Jumper said out of breath, "Killing me will only make my followers stronger. Killing me...will in fact fulfill the prophecy, whether you choose to believe it or not," Jumper concluded.

"There is nothing you can say to make me believe, and if you choose not to force me to, I will live on as I am." Lee-Der stated, charging at Jumper as he finished his statement.

Jumper prepared to dodge Lee-Der's attack.

But, in a single second, Jumper thought about what other Game Protectors and Glitches have said to him in the past. *"You are not the prophet, nor will you ever be. The prophet? Are you insane? How can you, a Ethite-Game-Protector ever be the prophet? Sure bud. Definitely you are the prophet. There is nothing you can say to make me believe, and if you choose not to force me to, I will live on as I am,"* Lee-Der's voice echoed in Jumper's mind.

Jumper proceeded to close his eyes, open them, and intentionally did not dodge Lee-Der.

The Death of Jumper at Watch Base 01, December 3, 2000

Jumper laid on the ground defeated, and Lee-Der walked over to Jumper, repeatedly punching him and beating him, until he had almost no life left. "Goodbye, prophet," Lee-Der mocked.

Lee-Der was then hit harshly on the jaw. It was Bolder.

"You Ethite scum!" Bolder held back no anger, no emotion, as he thrust his fist into Lee-Der's stomach.

Lee-Der snarled in pain.

"Jumper is the prophet!" Bolder screamed, "and if you do not believe so, I will take you down!" Bolder unsheathed an ax from his back and began swinging it at Lee-Der without thought. "He has performed every miracle, every teaching! He has brought together The Glitches and Game Protectors! Even still, you attempt to murder him. Not only once, but twice!" Bolder continued. Lee-Der grabbed Bolder's ax, and he yanked it from his hands. He then struck Bolder with it. Bolder stumbled back, half of his helmet shattered.

Bolder looked at Lee-Der with fire in his eyes. He then struck Lee-Der right in his face, sending him tumbling back, and he fell to the ground.

Bolder picked up his ax, and walked over to Lee-Der, "Say it. Say Jumper is the prophet," Bolder demanded.

"I will never believe the prophecy! I will never believe Jumper's words, nor yours!" Lee-Der argued.

Bolder was right about to kill Lee-Der, but then, in his mind, the words of Jumper were echoing: "On that day, you will see me laying on the ground. You will see him, see the man who is to kill me, and you will attack him without forethought. With a voice lashing out, you will cry out words of force. You will give the man no choice but to believe in me, and if he doesn't do so, you will prepare to kill him. You will make yourself no different from those who will be persecuting you."

Bolder looked over to Jumper. "Jumper..." Bolder said, dropping the ax. Weakness audible in his voice, as well as sadness. Bolder ran over to Jumper, crouching down to speak with him. Jumper, even with his death approaching, was not sad.

Jumper struggled to say, Jumper breathed in deeply, and then coughed, "I wish...there had been another way. I wish...it were possible to see all my effort and work...fulfilled, and finally...see all of this conflict end between The Game Protectors and Glitches. "At least, I get...to see my father again," Jumper said, slightly chuckling.

"What if you do not have to go? What if you get that retirement? Jumper! You can't leave us!" Bolder said with his voice quiet and weak, as well as cracking with sadness.

Jumper looked at Bolder and said "There ... is .... no ... other ... way..." Jumper's voice began to fade. Bolder thought for a moment, slowly moving his head to the sky. "The Prophecy...is fulfilled," Jumper said in a whisper, Bolder looked back at him. Jumper then closed his eyes.

Bolder Forgives Lee-Der, Watch Base 01, December 3, 2000

Bolder's eyes were closed. His breathing was uneven. Bolder then stood up, his back turned to Lee-Der. Bolder breathed in deeply, and then out. He opened his eyes, and just stood. Stood for a moment. He turned his head to the right, and then his full body. He walked towards Lee-Der, each step echoing a menacing tone. Lee-Der looked at Bolder with an expression of fright. Lee-Der shook, knowing he would be defenseless if

Bolder was to attack him. Lee-Der closed his eyes, expecting to see the heavens soon. The footsteps stopped. Lee-Der waited, but nothing happened. Reluctantly, Lee-Der slowly opened his eyes, and instead of a fist, he saw an open hand. Bolder's open hand. Lee-Der grabbed it, and he was yanked off the ground. Bolder then placed his hand on Lee-Der's left shoulder to help him stabilize, since Lee-Der's legs were still failing him.

Once stabilized, Lee-Der and Bolder looked at one another for a moment. "I-I forgive you," Bolder said, even though those words were difficult to say. Bolder let go of Lee-Der.

"I suppose I do too," Lee-Der said in reply, along with a smile that quickly disappeared. Lee-Der looked down to the ground, as Bolder took in the visuals around him. Another moment passed. "You know The Game Protectors and Glitches are not going to accept your beliefs," Lee-Der stated, lifting his head to reach Bolder's gaze.

Bolder looked back at Lee-Der. "I know." Bolder said in a quiet, and disappointed, tone as he nodded his head in agreement. Bolder looked down, although Lee-Der did not.

"What do you suppose we do?" Lee-Der looked at Bolder curiously.

"I...I" Bolder struggled to say, and then looked over his left shoulder. He took a glance at Jumper, Bolder eyes widened:

200

"I know what we do." Bolder said confidently as he turned his head back, facing Lee-Der.

The Fulfillment of the Prophecy, December 3, 2000

Suddenly, the bright, blue, vibrant, wonderful sky shattered into utter darkness. A loud crackle and boom erupted, shaking the terrain with an unpleasant shaking. With this, the Elder Game Protectors, Glitches, and Followers of Jumper ceased battle. They all were stunned and had their faces pointed toward the sky.

Then, roaring footsteps became audible as the sky continued to crackle with anger. Soon, a shadowy man appeared...it was Lee-Der.

"The Half-code is dead!" Lee-Der exclaimed. Bolder was by his right side, kneeling beside Lee-Der.

The Glitches and The Game Protectors celebrated together, bursting into cheerful yells and excited applause.

Lee-Der raised his hand high into the sky, his palm open, facing the crowd. The crowd immediately began to simmer down.

"There is no more need for bloodshed! For killing them will not remove their code from this land! I command that we exile them, throw them out like the garbage they are!" Lee-Der commanded. The Game Protectors and Glitches again erupted into a mess of loud cheers and applause.

The Exile of the Followers of Jumper, December 3, 2000

And so, the Followers of Jumper were exiled. Violently, they were pushed and pulled to the centerpiece of Watch Base 01, close to the marketplace area. During this process, The Glitches and Game Protectors beat on the Followers of Jumper, leaving scars and scratches all across their bodies. This resulted in their own programming and code to pour out, causing them to collapse onto the ground and even some of them to die.

In the front of the Exile Line was Bolder, being escorted by Lee-Der. Even with his bruises, cuts, and sores, Bolder carried Jumper's lifeless body.

Mobs of angry citizens proceeded to spit on and ridicule the Followers of Jumper as they passed; even mocking Jumper as he lay dead.

Eventually, they reached the centerpiece. Ahead was a portal to the game Crafting, and on both sides of the portal, were the Elder Game Protectors.

"Before this filth is exiled for crimes against The Developers, and against Watch Base 01, I must ask: was it worth it? Was your faith worth it?" Lead asked.

Bolder stayed quiet a moment, before deciding to speak: "Never in my life have I met a Game Protector to be more fond of. Jumper brought out a different side of me; he brought out emotion. He brought out care. I believe he truly was the prophet," Bolder admitted.

"Is that so?" Lead mocked.

"He cared 'bout all of us, and I'm pretty sure loved me. I didn't wanna admit it, but I think I loved him too. He never judged anyone. He also helped...no matter what," Racer said.

"And what of you, Eop? You have always been fond of going against the way," Lead asked.

"He did everything the prophecy said he would. And I do not mean "your" prophecy, but the true one. The original, untampered with, book. Whether you admit it or not, he united The Glitches and Game Protectors, proved himself by performing every single one of the miracles stated," Eop replied.

With every statement in Jumper's defense, everyone grew in anger.

"Cast them out already!" a citizen shouted.

"They are deluded!" another said.

"Liars!" one citizen screamed.

"Throw them out, like the beasts they are," Lead demanded.

The Glitches did so, with as much pain as they could administer to the Followers of Jumper.

Epilogue

The Mission of the Followers of Jumper Crafting, December 3, 2000

A circle of the Followers of Jumper was formed, with Bolder residing in the top-center of the congregation. "What'a we do now?" Racer asked quickly, her voice both out of breath and sounding nervous. Bolder was staring off, thinking. Bolder

211

looked back at Racer, "We do what Jumper would have wanted," Bolder said in a calm, and reassuring.

Eop interjected, "Those are good words, Bolder, but what exactly do they mean?" Eop said, his voice unsure, and his head tilting slightly to the left towards the end of the sentence. Bolder took another moment to think. "We honor him, honor Jumper. Allow the inhabitants of this world, and all the others, to know him, and what he did, and the teachings in which he shared with us."

Bolder looked at Eop, and then at the entire group. "However, this new faith shall not be the faith of those who persecuted us. We will not follow the methods in which they used. In our faith, those who choose to believe will be treated equally to those who do not," Bolder paused. "Secondly, we shall not force our beliefs onto anyone. This does not mean we cannot share our faith to non-believers, but it does mean that we will not persecute them, or harm them in any way. Even if they choose not to believe us," Bolder said, his voice calm, and quiet.

"What of Jumper's...body?" Eop asked wisely, his voice aged and crackling. Bolder looked around his surroundings, looking for a proper place to lay Jumper to rest. Eventually, Bolder's gaze met at a mountain, a ginormous, luxurious, and vast mountain. One that was fully covered with bright green grass, and a few stones. Bolder extended his arm and pointed his index finger. "That mountain! The green one off to the distance! That is where Jumper shall rest, and where his church will wake!" Bolder said, his voice booming.

The Separation of the Followers of Jumper Crafting, December 3, 2000

The Followers of Jumper soon made it to the top of the mountain and found an entrance to a cave. Bolder, whom had been carrying Jumper's body up the mountain, stared at the cave entrance. Bolder turned around, Jumper in his arms: "I shall go alone. I cannot risk any of you getting injured any further," Bolder stated, his voice calm and collected, with a hint of sorrow.

"Your voice....Bolder, is everything alright?" Skyia asked, trying to make sense of Bolder's tone.

"I am afraid not Skyia," Bolder breathed in, and thought about his words, just as Jumper used to. "If we are to spread the news of Jumper, we cannot do it as a group. If we were to do such an act, our enemies would easily be able to kill us all in one swift attack. Just as Byte and Lee-Der did when they betrayed us. I believe if we were to split up, not only would the news of Jumper spread faster, and wider, but our enemies would have a more difficult time tracking us down," Bolder stated. "I suppose I feel sorrow because...well, I care about this Squadron more than I could have ever fathomed. If any of you were to perish, and I was not there to save you, the guilt would overtake me," Bolder finished.

The Game Protectors smiled with joy, but were also sick with sadness.

"We will not let this faith dwindle Bolder. We shall not let our enemies win, and think they defeated us," Eop reassured. The Game Protectors then said their goodbyes and departed from each other. Bolder went into the cave.

The Burial of Jumper Crafting, December 3, 2000

It was pure darkness. Sounds of screeching bats clouded Bolder's hearing. When Bolder ultimately disturbed the bats enough, they came as a swarm and attacked him. Bolder raised his right arm to his head, and collapsed his head into his arm, barely having a grip on Jumper. He closed his eyes too. When the attack subsided, Bolder said to himself in a faint and agitated tone: "What are these foul creatures?" For he had never seen anything but a Game Protector or Glitch before.

Bolder continued walking down a narrow path, and eventually made it to a small dark room. Bolder proceeded to make a stack of flat rocks to lay Jumper on. This task was difficult, for since this room was further away from the previous hallway, barely any light illuminated the room. However, Bolder persevered, and crafted a makeshift bed to permanently lay Jumper down. Bolder did so with the upmost respect. He carefully and methodically laid Jumper down. Bolder made sure to prevent Jumper's body from hitting any objects, as if he were still alive. Once Jumper was laid down, Bolder collapsed to his knees. He bowed his head toward Jumper, and after he raised his head, he opened his hand and placed his palm on Jumper's forehead. "Thank...you." Bolder proceeded to say, his voice overwhelmed by sadness and pain, "You were the greatest man I have ever known," Bolder wept.

It was not even supposed to be possible, possible for a program to feel this complexity of emotions. Let alone do as Bolder did next: he cried. Bolder cried.

The End, Crafting, December 3, 2001

Bolder left the mountain, and did not turn back. He knew what his life had in store for him now, and he also knew to hold onto the things that he had learned. No longer shall he hide his true emotions from others. No longer will he allow others to be misjudged or mistreated just because of who they are. As long as he stays alive, he promised himself he would ensure that the Followers of Jumper never become as corrupt as the Elder Game Protectors. Nobody deserved to be treated poorly for what they believed in, or who they were. That is something Bolder, and the Followers of Jumper, will continue to preach.

Little did they know, Jumper would wake up from that cave...

ABOUT THE AUTHOR

Growing up in Florida, in many different counties throughout my life, I, Evan James Vaughan, always aspired to be a writer after being inspired by my friends to do so. I came up with the idea of *Jumper Origins* after being a Transformers fan most of my life. *Jumper Origins* has been through a lot of alterations throughout its creation, but after studying religions (mainly Christianity) I took inspiration to somewhat rewrite this story, into a reflection of the Bible, and what people's opinions and beliefs often are.

FACTS

Evan (mostly) does not like to read books.

Evan has made seven video game concepts,

and 30 book/movie concepts.

This is Evan's first ever book.

www.ingramcontent.com/pod-product-compliance
Lightning Source LLC
Chambersburg PA
CBHW050127030726
47505CB00007B/2076